STEPHANIE JAMES
Gamemaster

D0465308

Silhouette Desire

Published by Silhouette Books New York

America's Publisher of Contemporary Romance

SILHOUETTE BOOKS, a Simon & Schuster Division of
GULF & WESTERN CORPORATION
1230 Avenue of the Americas, New York, N.Y. 10020

ISBN: 0-671-44813-7

First Silhouette Books printing June, 1983

10 9 8 7 6 5 4 3 2 1

America's Publisher of Contemporary Romance

Printed in the U.S.A.

"I See Nothing Wrong in Making Love to a Business Partner."

The last word was breathed against her mouth and in the next instant his lips closed beguilingly over hers. She knew she should be protesting, that his attitude was all mixed up, that there *was* something wrong in making up the argument. With a shudder she relaxed languidly beneath his kiss.

It was slow and delicious, damp and invading, and she realized she'd had Joel's kiss in her head since last night. It had nibbled around the edge of her consciousness, sometimes reminding her of its presence forcefully, other times receding patiently into the background but always there. Always there. And tonight it was there in reality once more.

STEPHANIE JAMES

readily admits that the chief influence on her writing is her "lifelong addiction to romantic daydreaming." She has spent the last nine years living and working with her engineer husband in a wide variety of places, including the Caribbean, the Southeast and the Pacific Northwest. Ms. James currently resides in California.

Dear Reader:

Silhouette has always tried to give you exactly what you want. When you asked for increased realism, deeper characterization and greater length, we brought you Silhouette Special Editions. When you asked for increased sensuality, we brought you Silhouette Desire. Now you ask for books with the length and depth of Special Editions, the sensuality of Desire, but with something else besides, something that no one else offers. Now we bring you SILHOUETTE INTIMATE MOMENTS, true romance novels, longer than the usual, with all the depth that length requires. More sensuous than the usual, with characters whose maturity matches that sensuality. Books with the ingredient no one else has tapped: excitement.

There is an electricity between two people in love that makes everything they do magic, larger than life—and this is what we bring you in SILHOUETTE INTIMATE MOMENTS. Look for them wherever you buy books.

These books are for the woman who wants more than she has ever had before. These books are for you. As always, we look forward to your comments and suggestions. You can write to me at the address below:

Karen Solem
Editor-in-Chief
Silhouette Books
P.O. Box 769
New York, N.Y. 10019

Other Silhouette Books by Stephanie James

A Passionate Business
Dangerous Magic
Corporate Affair
Stormy Challenge
Velvet Touch
Lover in Pursuit
Renaissance Man
Reckless Passion
Price of Surrender
Affair of Honor
To Tame the Hunter

For my brother Steve, his wife Barb and their son Donnie. Congratulations on building one of the few miracles of the modern age: a real family that knows how to laugh.

Gamemaster

1

First impressions were always important, Shelley Banning reminded herself bracingly as she pushed open the door labeled Cassidy & Co. But she had to admit that seldom did quite so much ride on the outcome of how she handled the first few minutes of a business confrontation. She had to come across as dynamic, cool and utterly in charge of the situation.

And even if she managed to appear to be all of those things, it might not be enough to buy her the time she needed. She had the distinct feeling that a man like Joel Cassidy probably didn't sell anything, especially time, cheaply.

The door of the unimposing industrial building closed behind her, shutting out the heat of a Phoenix, Arizona, afternoon, and Shelley found herself staring at a roomful of pinball machines and video games in various stages of

repair and assembly. Racks of tools lined one wall, and
on the other were shelves of records, presumably for juke
boxes such as the one standing in the corner with its
mechanism exposed. Cassidy & Co. was an amusement-
machine business. Among other things, Shelley added
wryly as she glanced around the repair shop.

The place certainly didn't reflect the wealth of the man
who owned it, she concluded, but then mechanical repair
shops everywhere were probably much the same regardless of the money pulled in by the business.

"Damn!"

The muffled curse was followed almost immediately by
a loud, ominous crash. Both emanated from the room
adjoining the one in which Shelley was standing. Since
hers was decidedly empty of human life, she headed for
the doorway that opened on to the next.

She stepped through the second doorway into another
repair area much like the first except that in this one a
solitary man was struggling in obvious annoyance to raise
the long playboard of a colorfully painted pinball machine.

The first thing she noticed about the man was the pelt
of flame-red hair. It was thick and cut long enough in
back to brush the collar of the faded blue work shirt he
was wearing. Shelley's hazel eyes narrowed speculatively
as she studied the fluid shift of muscles under the shirt as
he stood with his back toward her and raised the
playboard back into position.

Open, it revealed the intricate electromechanical work-
ings of a pinball machine, and from the way the redheaded man warily eyed the prop stick, Shelley had a
hunch the heavy board, lined with wires and relays, had
just come crashing down unexpectedly, probably barely
missing that red head.

"Excuse me, I'm looking for Mr. Joel Cassidy," Shelley

announced firmly. "I understood he could be found here today."

"What the hell . . . !" Clearly surprised at the sound of her soft, slightly throaty voice, the pinball mechanic raised his head rather abruptly. His elbow swiped the unsteady prop stick, and once again the heavy playboard crashed back into place.

The man was quick, Shelley acknowledged silently. She watched with interest as he managed to get his hands and head out of the path of danger in the nick of time. His vocabulary seemed limited, if colorful. The muttered oath he was growling as he turned to face his visitor was not printable.

"Mr. Cassidy," he informed her dryly, "can indeed be found here today. The question of whether he will be found dead or merely permanently maimed remains open, however."

"You're Joel Cassidy?" Shelley knew a distinct sense of shock as the steel blue of his eyes met hers. With barely concealed astonishment, she quickly raked the lean, wiry, masculine figure clad in faded, low-riding jeans, a pair of calfskin boots and the work shirt. Only the boots betrayed a hint of the money Joel Cassidy was reputed to control. They were of supple leather and superbly crafted, and Shelley knew they had cost a fortune.

As she was adjusting to the unexpected image in front of her, Cassidy made a slight movement to set down a pair of pliers he had been gripping in one square, strong hand, and another bit of luxury emerged as the cuff of the work shirt shifted to reveal a very thin, very expensive gold watch on his left wrist.

It wasn't enough. The watch and the boots didn't suffice to counter the image of pinball mechanic. This was the man who held the future of Ackerly Manufacturing in his grasp? The man who was unknowingly in a position to do so much for her own career? He just wasn't what she had anticipated, Shelley thought in confusion.

Joel Cassidy should have been dressed in a pin-stripe suit, a silk tie and a shirt that was only sent to a French cleaners for laundering. He should have been suave, dark-haired and seated behind a mahogany desk downtown. Good heavens! Even Ackerly Manufacturing, a company in such dire straits it was on the verge of bankruptcy, housed its president better than this!

But when she met the steel-colored blue of his eyes, Shelley was forced to admit there might be more to the man than his attire suggested. There was cool intelligence in those eyes and an underlying perception that she would do well to acknowledge from the start. Men didn't become as financially successful as Joel Cassidy just by being good-natured, easygoing, good old boys.

He was thirty-eight or thirty-nine years old, Shelley knew, and the first hint of silver was already dusting the heavy red hair. Some of the crinkling lines around the eyes and the etched brackets on either side of the firm mouth spoke of laughter, but most of them spoke of experience gained the hard way.

Joel Cassidy was not a handsome man, but there was a strength, a self-confidence in him that made itself known on a fundamental level. Shelley's senses reacted to that subtle force even while she catalogued the aggressive nose, sharp, lean planes of jaw and chin and the quiet authority with which he stood facing her. He might not have dressed the part today, but she would do well to remember the importance of the role he was to play in her life. No, she would not underestimate Joel Cassidy. She never underestimated anyone who wielded as much financial power as this man did.

"I'm Joel Cassidy," he agreed with a faint nod as he swept Shelley with an assessing glance.

Shelley took a deep breath and lifted her chin determinedly. "I'm Shelley Banning from Mason Wells & Associates. I'm here to speak to you on behalf of one of our clients. I realize you're busy," she added, flicking a glance at the waiting pinball machine, "but I'd appreciate it if you could spare a few minutes to talk to me."

"Talk to you about what?" he asked calmly, one red brow arching quizzically.

"Money. A hundred thousand dollars, to be precise."

Cassidy whistled soundlessly. "I'm nearly always available to discuss that kind of money. Have a seat." He indicated a stool located near a workbench nearby. With a last appraising glance, he turned back to the pinball machine and once again raised the playboard.

Behind him, Shelley frowned uncertainly and then shrugged, walked across the bare concrete floor and perched herself on the wooden stool. Hooking the heels of her burnished leather pumps over a rung, she adjusted the narrow skirt of her yellow linen suit. She regarded Joel Cassidy as he bent over his machine and began fiddling with an interior mechanism.

He was no longer looking at her, but she wasn't fooled for a minute. The blue eyes hadn't missed an inch of her figure or her attire when they had swept over her a moment earlier. Shelley found herself wondering briefly what he had thought of her and then dismissed the question. What did she care? She was here to do business with the man, not seduce him!

In any event, she reminded herself on a note of inner laughter, she was hardly the seductive type. Everything from the short cut of her toast-brown hair, which was softly and sleekly shaped into the nape of her neck, to the crisp lines of the yellow suit, with its close-fitting jacket and white tie-collared blouse, spelled business.

The hazel of her eyes was a blend of green and blue that could mirror a variety of emotions, from cool disdain to warm laughter, and always reflected her underlying intelligence. The face, framed by the short curve of toast-colored hair, was marked by an energy and animation that often made the onlooker forget the lack of any real beauty. It was an interesting face, not a beautiful one, with its firm line of nose and jaw. The hint of sensuality in the fullness of her lower lip somehow blended nicely with the feminine strength, making a promise of warmth just beneath the surface.

The yellow suit fit well over the fullness of rounded breasts and hips that had more of a curve than Shelley would have liked. It was a fullness that she fought valiantly and continually with a never-ending diet. A difference of only five pounds was enough to mark the border between rounded and plump in her mind, and she defended that border zealously. There were, unfortunately, too many occasions when she abandoned the fight temporarily.

"Okay, Miss Shelley Banning, what are you selling? Swampland in Florida? Dry oil wells in Oklahoma? How are you going to entice me to part with a hundred thou?" Joel asked with apparent curiosity as he hovered over the pinball game.

"You've already parted with it," she murmured politely. "I'm here to ask you to stay parted from it a while longer than you had intended, that's all."

He lifted his eyes from the switch he was adjusting, and his gaze collided with hers. "Who did you say you represented?" he asked very calmly.

"Mason Wells & Associates. It's an accounting firm here in Phoenix," she responded quietly, aware of a sensation of being pinned like a yellow butterfly.

"And your client?" he prodded, resting on his elbows as he watched her from under the raised playboard.

"Ackerly Manufacturing," she told him with a bravado she was far from feeling. Then she waited.

"I see." He nodded, glancing back inside his machine. *"That* hundred grand."

"Yes, that hundred thousand."

"Would you hand me that wrench behind you?" He didn't look up.

Shelley's eyes narrowed. Was the man going to play games with her? She stifled a small exclamation of irritation and glanced around for the wrench. It was lying on the workbench, and she picked it up. Sliding off the stool, she walked forward to stand across from him on the opposite side of the pinball machine. Wordlessly, she held out the tool.

"Thanks."

Again, she waited. Shelley wanted his full attention. He applied the wrench carefully and precisely and then handed it back to her without looking up.

"Phil Ackerly died two months ago," he finally pointed out. "The money was due three months ago."

"I'm aware of that. I've just been assigned the Ackerly account, and I've been going through the books. That's why I'm here to see you today, Mr. Cassidy." She must be steady, businesslike, certain about the direction in which she was going. Silently, Shelley kept up the positive-thinking lecture. No one had said convincing someone to give up a hundred thousand dollars was going to be easy.

"What, exactly, are you asking me to do?" The question was conversational in nature. Joel appeared more interested in a sticking relay inside the machine than in her answer.

"I'm asking you to give Ackerly Manufacturing another six months before you demand repayment, and I'm asking you to let me schedule that repayment in installments."

He did look up at that, a lazy grin slicing across his hard features to reveal strong white teeth, not all of which,

Shelley found herself noting, were perfectly straight. There was an unexpectedly charming crookedness to one on the left side. That she'd even been aware of such a tiny detail annoyed her.

"You're kidding" was all he said. The blue eyes flared briefly with real humor.

Shelley's fingers tightened as she unconsciously curled them over the edge of the machine housing. "I'm not joking, Mr. Cassidy. Ackerly Manufacturing is on the brink of a long slide into bankruptcy. I'm going to save it, but I'll need your cooperation to do so."

"I'm in the fun-and-games business, Miss Banning," he drawled meaningfully, "not the charitable contributions field."

"Will you at least listen to what I have to say? I promise that in the end you won't lose. You'll merely be deferring the payback."

"Is this the part where you offer me your body in exchange for my agreement not to press for the money?" he inquired interestedly. The blue eyes swept down to the curve of her breast, and Shelley had to resist a sudden urge to step backward. It was as if he'd actually reached out and touched her.

She should have been prepared for such a jibe, but it took her by surprise nonetheless, perhaps because her own mind had been so totally on business. She covered the moment of shock with a flashing glance of utter disdain, but nothing could halt the rush of red into her cheeks. Lord! She was thirty years old and had learned something about the occasionally uncouth ways of the business world long ago. Surely she wasn't going to let this man embarrass her so readily.

"No, Mr. Cassidy—"

"Joel," he corrected mildly. "Call me Joel. Something tells me we're fated to be on a first-name basis."

"No, Joel," she said very evenly, taking a grip on her

poise, "this isn't the part where I offer you my body, and I recommend you don't hold your breath waiting for that particular bargain. I can guarantee it isn't in the offing. I'm here to talk business, and I would appreciate it if you would be so kind as to pull yourself away from that machine long enough to hear me out. It is, after all, a great deal of money we're talking about!"

"*My* money," he emphasized.

"Your money," she affirmed gamely. Why was she letting him bait her? She had to hold her own against this man or everything would be lost. "If you'll listen to my plans, I can show you how you'll get your money back."

"That money was secured by certain Ackerly Manufacturing assets," he murmured. "I'll get it back one way or another. Even if the company goes into bankruptcy."

"I'm here to convince you to wait."

"That loan was made to a friend, Phil Ackerly, not to his son. Now that Phil's dead, I don't see why I should wait for repayment. Personally, I don't give a damn what happens to Ackerly Manufacturing now that Phil's gone."

"You may not care about the future of the company, but there are a great many people who do, including other creditors and a lot of employees! Demanding repayment right now will be all it takes to push the company over the brink. I need a little time, Mr. Cassidy. Joel," she amended quickly, seeing that he was about to correct her again.

"You need the time? I'm curious, Shelley. What's in this for you?"

He did have a way of getting to the heart of the matter, she admitted ruefully. Perhaps that was one of the talents required for getting rich.

"I told you, I inherited the account from my predecessor at Mason Wells, who recently retired. It's my job to try to straighten out the company."

"As the firm's accountant, you're not required to save

it, merely to make certain that the financial records are
nice and neat," he said calmly. "Would you hand me that
screwdriver over there on the bench?"

Shelley's mouth tightened for an instant, and then she
gave in and walked over to retrieve the screwdriver. "A
good accountant is in a position to counsel a firm like
Ackerly when it is in a difficult financial position. I want to
help the company, and I think I can do it."

"Why?" He took the screwdriver and went back to
work.

"Because it's my job!" she gritted, losing patience
rapidly.

"It's not your job to come pleading to the firm's
creditors." He didn't raise his head as he spoke, electing
to concentrate on the task at hand.

"I'm making it my job!"

"Why?"

"Because I am! That's why!"

"You sleeping with Phil's son? What's his name?
David? No, Dean, isn't it?"

The remainder of her patience went up in a puff of
smoke. "Mr. Cassidy, if you don't pull yourself out of that
machine and give me a little of your no doubt valuable
time, I will personally see to it that the prop stick suffers
another unexpected accident. This time you may not get
out of the way quickly enough to avoid having that board
put a picturesque scar on your head!"

The steel-blue eyes lifted assessingly to her flaming
hazel gaze and taut features. For an instant, he didn't
move, studying her intently. Then wry humor flickered
behind the auburn lashes and tugged at the corners of his
mouth. Very carefully, as if afraid of triggering the
"accident" with a too-hasty move, he straightened.
Gingerly, he lowered the playboard back into place,
never taking his eyes off Shelley.

"There," he said gently, turning toward her, "now that

you've cowed me with threats of physical violence, perhaps you'll join me in a cup of coffee? I promise to give you my full attention."

The momentary anger dissolved, leaving Shelley disgusted with her loss of control. She would never get anywhere unless she maintained control of herself and of the situation. "Thank you. A cup of coffee would be appreciated."

With a nod, he led her toward another workbench on the opposite side of the room. At one end, a coffee machine and several dirty cups reposed.

"Don't worry, I've got some plastic cups," he murmured, seeing her uncertain glance at the used mugs. He opened a cupboard and drew out a styrofoam cup. "Cream?"

"No, thanks," she said automatically. A professional dieter learned to always say "no" to that particular question. Wordlessly, she accepted the cup of dark, steaming brew.

"You may change your mind about the cream. Greg makes the stuff the way he likes it, which is strong, to say the least."

"Greg?"

"One of my men. He's out on a call at the moment. Running this business is a lot like being a doctor. We're on call twenty-four hours a day." He sipped cautiously at his own mug.

Shelley frowned curiously. "Why is that?"

"The machines are in various bars, restaurants and arcades only as long as the owner of the location wants them. If the guy who owns the tavern doesn't get good service from me, he's likely to give his business to another operator. It's a hell of an incentive for Cassidy & Co. to provide 'round-the-clock repair and maintenance."

"Someone has to get out of bed at midnight if the

video game in one of your locations goes down or the juke box gets broken?" she demanded, glancing around at the roomful of tools and machines.

"Yup. That's why I hire people like Greg and Mac. In the beginning, I was the only one available to get out of a warm bed in the middle of the night. Played merry hell with my social life," he added a little too politely, blue eyes glinting.

"I can imagine," she retorted with what she hoped was a total lack of interest. Striving for a more neutral topic, she asked quickly, "Do you still have many of those traditional pinball games in the arcades and taverns? I thought the new video games had become the rage."

"They have. I've pulled in most of the old-fashioned pinball machines and replaced them with the videos. That one I was working on when you started threatening to assassinate me with it is out of a truck stop. There were a few traditionalists still patronizing the place, so I left it there, but the owner finally said he wanted one of the newer games."

"What in the world do you do with an old pinball machine?" she asked.

"I recondition them, take out the coin chutes and sell them to private parties who want one for their home recreation room. That's what I was doing with that one." He nodded toward the machine he'd been working on when she'd arrived.

"I see." She took a gulp of her coffee, trying to figure out what to say next. How was she going to get the conversation back on track?

"Now that I've given you this brief glimpse into the life of an amusement-machine route operator," he went on dryly, "why don't you tell me a little more about the exciting world of accounting?"

"Such as?" she asked warily.

"Such as why you've undertaken the task of championing Ackerly Manufacturing," he retorted firmly.

"You keep implying there's something personal in it for me," she sighed.

"And I'll go on implying it until I find out what that something personal is. Come now, Shelley, if you're asking me to forgo a hundred grand indefinitely, the least you can do is be honest about where you fit into the picture." He lounged back against the workbench, watching her coolly.

Shelley hesitated, unsure how much to tell him, and then decided there was nothing wrong with the truth. "I want to use Ackerly to make my name in the consulting world," she finally said quietly. "It's my golden opportunity to gain a reputation as a consulting accountant who can handle situations such as impending bankruptcy. I have no intention of growing old behind a desk at Mason Wells & Associates. I want to start my own firm one of these days and specialize in helping firms in trouble."

"That's your sole motivation?" he persisted.

She shut her eyes in brief, controlled irritation. "My sole motivation."

"You're not sleeping with Dean Ackerly?"

She turned to face him boldly. "If I were, it sure as hell wouldn't be any of your business!"

"I disagree. When there's this much money involved, a man likes to know all the details."

"You didn't seem overly concerned about details when you loaned Phil Ackerly that money a year ago!" she pointed out accusingly.

"Phil was a friend, and I knew he needed the money. Besides, I owed it to him." Joel lifted one shoulder dismissively. "He was the one who insisted on securing the loan with company assets."

"You *owed* it to him!" Shelley stared at him uncomprehendingly.

"He gave me a loan when I needed it to get started in business several years ago."

"He loaned you a hundred thousand dollars several years ago?" She was getting more and more confused.

"It was only five thousand, but at the time that much money was as out of my reach as a hundred grand was for him last year. Everything's relative, Shelley. You know that."

"Did you pay back the five?"

"Of course. Within six months." He looked surprised she should even ask.

"So you made the loan last year more as a personal favor than as a business deal?"

"The favor was to Phil. It became an outstanding, uncollected debt as far as I was concerned the day he died and his son took over the firm."

She drew a breath. "Then how about continuing to think of it as a favor to Phil's heir for another few months?"

He grinned. "Not a chance."

"You don't like Dean Ackerly?"

"I've never met the man."

"Then why not give him a chance for Phil's sake?"

"I might have been susceptible to that sort of appeal if Dean had come back from California last year when Phil first realized he was in trouble financially. As it was, he seems to have ignored his father and the business until he inherited the firm. He didn't show up when Phil needed him, so why should I care what happens to him now?"

"You're being unfair, Joel. You don't know enough about the situation to judge Dean's actions," she told him earnestly.

"Do you? You just recently inherited the account. How

much do you know about the family situation?" he growled challengingly.

Shelley had the grace to blush. "It's not my business to pry into such matters. I'm only concerned with trying to salvage the firm."

"In order to establish a reputation for yourself," he concluded.

"Is there anything wrong with that?" Her eyes met his determinedly. "You've certainly done all right for yourself. What objection do you have to others trying to do the same?"

"None. As long as they don't try to use my money to do it with."

"I'm not using your money to do it!"

"Sure you are. Asking me to defer collection on that loan is as good as asking me for another loan. Do you have any idea what the interest is on a hundred thousand dollars these days?" he asked mildly.

"You'll get interest on your money," she assured him quickly. "I'll make sure it's paid back with interest."

"How much interest?" he inquired.

For the first time since she had begun the conversation, Shelley allowed herself to hope. "That's something we could negotiate," she began tentatively.

"No we can't. I'd want the prime rate at least," he retorted easily.

"You gave the money interest-free to Phil Ackerly. It's asking a lot to suddenly start charging the prime rate on it," she murmured.

"The prime rate on my money is only the start of what I'd ask if I let you talk me into extending the loan." He reached out and removed her now-empty cup from her fingers and tossed it into an overfull trash container. Then his gaze slid back to confront her questioning look. "I'd want to be kept completely briefed on the progress you

were making or not making on saving Ackerly Manufacturing. That would mean regular, totally honest reports.
I'd want a detailed, written plan of how you intended to
go about the salvage operation in the first place, and I'd
want the right to contribute to that plan or veto the parts I
didn't like. I'd want Dean Ackerly to know he can't ride
on his father's friendship with me. I'm like the bank: I'm
to be paid off regardless of what happens. I'd want total
involvement every step of the way and the right to call
the whole thing off if I decide it's a hopeless task trying to
keep Ackerly out of bankruptcy. That's what I'd want in
addition to the prime interest rate on my hundred grand,
Shelley Banning."

She stared at him. She'd known, of course, that the
easygoing pinball-mechanic image was something of a
façade, but she hadn't quite expected the blue-eyed,
hard-driving business devil underneath. "I think I'm
beginning to see why you've been so, uh, successful in
your business ventures, Mr. Cassidy," she finally observed.

He continued to lounge against the workbench. "You
didn't think it was going to be simple or easy, did you?"

"No," she admitted.

"Would you agree to the terms of such a deal,
Shelley?" he pursued a little too gently.

"I don't have a great deal of choice in the matter, do
I?" Her lips turned downward ruefully. "Are you saying
that if I do agree to your terms, you'll lay off Ackerly
Manufacturing until I can get the company back on its
feet?"

"I'm saying I'd be willing to discuss such terms over
dinner this evening," he replied quietly.

Shelley went very still. "I'm sure you have much more
interesting ways of spending your evening," she tried
carefully. Every sense was painfully alert now, not just

her business-oriented ones but the much more fundamental, elemental feminine ones, too.

"The idea of letting you control a hundred thousand dollars of my money over the next few months suddenly puts you at the top of my list of interesting dinner guests," he said, smiling. But there was a cool, flickering assessment in the steel depths of his eyes. Shelley could almost feel the probing glance as if it were tangible in nature.

"We can discuss business this afternoon right here in your office," she said evenly. "Why do you want to do it over dinner?"

"Because I want to find out more about you, Shelley Banning. Not only because I'm thinking of letting you talk me into extending that loan but"—he broke off and then finished coolly—"because I think you and I have some things in common."

"I doubt that," she retorted with conviction.

"Let's find out, shall we?"

"Mr. Cassidy—" she began firmly.

"Joel. I've already told you once."

"Joel, I'm not going to be part of any business deal we arrive at," she stated emphatically.

"No," he agreed surprisingly, and then spoiled the effect by going on deliberately, "but if I'm right, what we may have in common transcends any single business venture."

"What in the world do you mean by that?" She glared at him sharply, wary and uncertain.

"I think we're both a pair of hustlers, Shelley," he drawled dangerously. "You intrigue me because I think you're a lady after my own heart. It takes nerve to walk into a man's life and ask him to forgo a hundred thousand dollars. I like that kind of nerve. If you want to come to terms, have dinner with me this evening. Otherwise, forget the whole thing."

She bit back an instinctive denial. What did she have to lose? Surely she could handle this man over dinner. "You drive a hard bargain, Joel."

"You ain't seen nothin' yet," he promised cheerfully. "I'll pick you up around seven. And wear something nice. We won't be going to any of my amusement-game locations!"

"Meaning those locations aren't particularly nice?" she retorted.

He grinned, revealing the engagingly crooked tooth. "Meaning I want to keep my mind on doing business with you, not one of my location owners. Dealing with a charming little hustler such as yourself will require my full attention, I think."

Abruptly, Shelley made her decision. Dinner was a small price to pay if she got what she wanted from him. Reaching into her leather shoulder bag, she withdrew her card and a pen. Hastily, she jotted down her address on the back of the pasteboard and handed it to him. "I'll be ready at seven, and I'll have an outline of my plans for Ackerly to go over with you at dinner," she told him assertively, as if the idea of having dinner had been hers.

He raised one red brow admiringly as he took the card. "As I said, a born hustler. It's going to be interesting working with you, Shelley Banning."

"When it comes to hustling, Joel Cassidy," she returned with acid sweetness, "I think you take the prize!"

"Only because I'm a little older than you and I've had a hell of a lot more experience," he said, chuckling.

Unable to think of a suitably quelling reply, Shelley turned on her heel and walked out of the shop without glancing back.

2

He arrived one minute before seven, but Shelley was ready for him. She'd given up on trying to second-guess the kind of place he might take her or the way he would be dressed. The white southwestern-style skirt she had chosen was full and flounced at the hem, and she had paired it with a long-sleeved black silk blouse trimmed with small turquoise buttons. Around her waist Shelley had looped a wide silver and turquoise belt. Black, high-heeled sandals and silver earrings completed the look, which she hoped was both chic and remotely cool. As she'd finished brushing her toast-colored hair into a light, soft curve, Shelley had taken stock of her own reflection in the mirror.

"You are *not* a hustler," she'd told herself out loud. "Hustlers are people who make their money in pinball arcades and slick real estate deals. Hustlers are people who insist on making a pass at a woman over dinner before they'll talk business with her. Joel Cassidy is a hustler. And the pass, when it occurs, will be brushed off as if it weren't worth noticing."

It was with such sentiments in her head that she opened the door at one minute before seven to reveal Joel Cassidy, who definitely did not look like a pinball mechanic. He still wore the thin gold watch, but the denims and coarse cotton work shirt had been replaced by a cream-colored jacket and tan slacks. The hand-sewn leather shoes were every bit as expensive looking as the boots had been earlier in the day. The pelt of red hair was combed into neat, gleaming order. In spite of her warnings to herself, Shelley experienced the same tug on her senses, the same awareness of his casual power, that she had known that afternoon in the shop. The knowledge annoyed her for some obscure reason.

"Won't you come in?" she made herself say politely, holding the door. "A glass of wine before we leave?" Anticipating an answer in the affirmative, she was already moving away from him, heading for the kitchen.

"Thank you," he murmured behind her. "That would be nice."

Shelley poured the chilled Napa Valley Chenin Blanc quickly, vitally aware of the way Joel was gliding around her living room, examining the surroundings. When she walked out of the cheerful, modern kitchen, she found he'd completed his perusal of the low, comfortable Spanish décor of her condominium and had come to a halt beside the puzzle table. Hearing her step on the brightly colored kitchen tile floor, Joel glanced up expectantly. Across the room she could see the assessing, anticipatory light in his blue eyes. Once again, Shelley reminded herself to play the game cautiously.

"You haven't made much progress on your puzzle," he remarked, taking the Chenin Blanc from her hand. He let his fingers lightly graze hers as he did so, and Shelley knew it was no accident. Irritated with herself for being so aware of the warmth in his casual touch, she took a determined sip of her own wine and contrived to step away from him on the pretext of glancing down at the puzzle.

"I just opened it up last night," she explained easily, surveying the thousand interlocking pieces that eventually were to go together to form a scene of Venice. "I'm addicted to them, I'm afraid. Some people watch television; I do puzzles."

He was suddenly close again, standing at her elbow to look down at the table. "I don't think I've done one since I was eight years old. Looks hopeless."

"There are tricks and patterns you learn after a while," she told him offhandedly, idly reaching down to fit a small piece into the gondola emerging in the left-hand corner of the scene.

"There are tricks and patterns to everything, aren't there?" Joel smiled with not-so-subtle provocation. "I'm looking forward to finding out which ones you'll be using."

"Which ones I'll be using to help save Ackerly Manufacturing?" Shelley slanted him a deliberate glance.

"Which ones you'll be using on me," he growled softly in a voice that, Shelley was learning, had a way of sending shivers along her nerve endings.

"I'm doing business with you, Joel. I'm not playing games." She wanted to make that point very clear.

"My dear little hustler," he murmured, downing the last sip of his wine, "haven't you learned yet that there is no real difference between the two?"

The restaurant was elegant, continental and located in the wealthy community of Scottsdale, on the edge of Phoenix. Shelley's heart sank as Joel parked his white

Maserati in the lot. She slid out of the white leather seat with a reluctance that couldn't quite be hidden as Joel opened the door for her.

"Something wrong?" he asked with unexpected concern.

"Oh, no! It's a lovely place," Shelley hastened to assure him. She was there on business, wasn't she? It took willpower to conduct business under any circumstances. Tonight it would just take a bit more than she had planned, that was all. Lifting her chin bravely, she allowed him to guide her into the plushly decorated restaurant.

"Are you sure you don't mind eating here?" he demanded in a low voice as the huge menus were handed to them. He leaned across the table, forehead creased in growing consternation.

"I told you, it's delightful," she insisted, opening the menu to the list of salads. The trick would be not to open it past this particular page, she decided firmly. Between keeping her mind on business and refusing to read through the descriptions of the various specialties, she ought to be able to survive the evening.

"Look, if you'd rather go somewhere else, Shelley," Joel broke in a moment later, "I won't mind at all."

"This place is fine. One of the best in the valley," she stated resolutely.

"That was my impression, too," he returned dryly. "But you look as if you're being led to the scaffold."

She glanced up, her most charming smile firmly in place. "That's what thinking about business does to me, I expect."

"Then don't think about it." He broke off as the waiter arrived for their order. "What would you like, Shelley?"

"I'll have the hearts of palm and pine nut salad," she said, smiling gamely up at the waiter, who dutifully jotted down her order and waited expectantly. "That will be all, thank you."

The man blinked in surprise but recovered quickly and turned to take Joel's order. Joel ignored him. "What else are you going to have, Shelley?" he prodded.

"Just the salad, thank you."

He stared at her. "Just the salad! Are you joking? I take you to the best restaurant in the area and you order just a salad? Don't be ridiculous!" He put out a hand and plucked the menu from her grasp. Then he turned to the waiter. "We'll have the *pâté maison* with French bread, the hearts of palm and pine nut salad, the snapper *en papillote,* wild rice and the spinach soufflé. For dessert," he continued with a hard look at Shelley's stricken expression, "we'll have the chocolate fondue with strawberries." He handed over the menus without taking his stern gaze off Shelley. "Just a salad," he muttered chidingly.

"You have no right to play the masterful type when it comes to the issue of my food," she hissed in a barely audible voice.

An engaging grin replaced Joel's condemning look. "Does that mean I *can* play the masterful role when it comes to other issues?"

"Stop teasing me. I happen to be on a diet," she explained austerely.

"Don't worry, you'll burn off lots of calories trying to save Ackerly Manufacturing," he shot back dismissively. "Besides, you don't need to diet. I like you the way you are." The blue eyes moved with satisfaction over her figure.

"What you think of me hardly matters," she replied aloofly, warming under the impact of that glance. "What counts is what you think of my plans for Ackerly."

"So tell me how you're going to stop the slide into

bankruptcy," he prompted agreeably. Too agreeably, Shelley thought. Nevertheless, she launched into a synopsis of her plans.

"The first rule in this kind of crisis management is to nail down all the cash. Ackerly will have to reduce overhead, push collection of receivables, sell off inventory and turn assets into cash."

"And put off creditors indefinitely," he added helpfully.

"Not indefinitely," Shelley protested. "But we will have to plan a different payback schedule."

"Hasn't Ackerly got bank loans to worry about, too?" Joel asked as the pâté arrived. He spread the rich stuff onto a slice of French bread and pushed it into Shelley's hand.

"Yes, unfortunately." She stared helplessly down at the pâté.

"Are you going to ask the bank to defer collecting its money the way you're asking me to do?" he inquired in amusement, spreading pâté on a chunk of bread for himself.

Shelley sighed. "I'm approaching you because I don't think I'll be able to convince the bank to lay off." The thought was depressing enough to make her take a bite of the pâté and bread. God! It was good.

"I see." Joel watched the delicious morsel disappear neatly into her mouth and smiled with approval.

"Does that smile indicate you're willing to go along with my plans?" Shelley asked hopefully, unconsciously taking another bite of the pâté.

"Keep talking," he murmured, not answering the question.

And she did, all the way through the pâté, the salad and the wonderful snapper. By the time the fondue pot full of chocolate and liqueur arrived, Shelley was beyond thinking about the food. She simply ate with complete pleasure, concentrating mentally on building her case for the salvaging of Ackerly Manufacturing. Joel listened with flattering attention, but for the life of her, she couldn't be sure what he was thinking.

"And if you pull this off successfully, you figure you'll be on your way to setting up your own consulting firm?" he concluded as he dipped the last strawberry into the melted chocolate and bit into it.

Shelley nodded, not wanting to get into an extended discussion of that side of the matter. She didn't like being called a hustler.

He swallowed the strawberry and nodded decisively. "Okay, Shelley Banning, you've got yourself a deal. Under the terms I outlined this afternoon."

Startled by the unexpectedly quick capitulation, Shelley stared at him, lips slightly parted in astonishment, before she rushed to accept the offer.

"Thank you, Joel. The terms are acceptable. Ackerly Manufacturing will be most appreciative, I assure you."

"I don't give a damn about Ackerly's appreciation," he informed her smoothly as he got to his feet and put out a strong hand to guide her out of her chair. "You're the one I'll be holding personally responsible for the success of your scheme."

"Me!" She shot him a covert look.

"You. Let's go back to your place and work on that puzzle." He smiled dangerously down at her wary expression. "Naturally, I'm going to hold you accountable for the success of this deal," he explained patiently. "You don't think I got where I am today by being a nice guy, do you?"

"Do I hear a threat buried somewhere in that sentence?" she demanded spiritedly as he helped her into the Maserati.

"The trick to handling threats, Shelley, is to pretend you're not the least intimidated by them," he advised helpfully as he turned the key in the ignition and backed the sleek car expertly out of the parking space.

"Another pearl of wisdom from an older and wiser hustler?" she drawled, aware she was letting herself be drawn into his banter but unable to resist. Sure of his agreement, she was suddenly in a very good frame of mind. She had accomplished what she had set out to do today, and she was now free to proceed with her plans. The future promised a great deal, and she was not about to let his teasing threats alarm her at this juncture.

"I'm full of such pearls of wisdom." He chuckled softly. "Want to hear some more?"

"I don't think so. The evening is too nice to spoil with lectures." She rolled down the window to inhale the warm desert breeze as the Maserati sped through downtown Phoenix.

"Pleased with yourself, hmmm?" He slid a speculative glance across at her profile.

"As pleased as you probably were with yourself when you pulled off the real estate deal with that huge California conglomerate a few months ago," she allowed easily.

"You know about that, huh? I didn't realize it was public knowledge."

"I did a little checking into your business life before I approached you this afternoon," she admitted negligently. "I wanted to know what I was tackling before I tried to talk you into my plan."

"Wise of you, honey, very wise. Did you check far enough, I wonder?"

"Far enough to find out what?" She wasn't quite sure how to tell him not to call her "honey." She didn't want to inject any animosity into the rather enjoyable atmosphere that was now filling the car. Well, if he did it again, she would say something polite about the presumption. When you were this satisfied with yourself, you didn't want to go out of your way to be rude to others, she thought with an inner smile. The success of the evening was as pleasant to her senses as the dinner had been.

"Never mind," he purred blandly. "I'll see to it that you find out whatever you need to know about me as we go along."

He didn't give her a chance to choose between inviting him into her home or bidding him good night on the doorstep. When she stepped over her threshold, Joel was right behind her, closing the door behind them very firmly.

"A glass of cognac before you leave?" she offered calmly, not really alarmed by his quietly growing aggression. There was, after all, nothing she ought to fear. And she had been expecting a pass, hadn't she?

"Thought you'd never ask." The hard line of his mouth curved upward whimsically as he faced her.

"I'll be right back. Have a seat." She kept it light, easy, very polite. Two business associates sharing a drink to salute the close of a deal. Her step as she moved off to the kitchen was firm.

He was sitting at the glass-topped puzzle table when she returned with the snifters of cognac. Two of the carved, straight-backed, Spanish-style chairs had been drawn up to it, and he rose with an unconscious grace to seat her in the one across from him.

"I can't help wondering if it's doing business with me which has put you in such a charming mood or the fact that you ate a decent meal tonight," he said, inhaling the aromatic fumes of the cognac as he held the rounded glass cupped in his hands.

"Please don't mention the food!" she begged, eyeing him across the rim of her glass. "You were wicked to lead me into the path of temptation like that."

"How long have you been dieting?" he asked, grinning.

"Most of my life," she groaned wryly. "It's a never-ending battle. Oh, look, here's another piece of sky." Bending forward slightly, she slipped the interlocking piece into place with satisfaction. "This is a tricky one because some of the sky is almost the same color as the water."

"Tricky, all right." He nodded solemnly, fingering a piece of gondola.

"Now don't make fun of my choice of amusements just because you're more accustomed to the flash and dazzle of those video games!" She glanced around for another chunk of sky, already getting caught up in the peculiar addiction of finding just one more piece.

He was watching her, not the scene of Venice, but she determinedly ignored his intent scrutiny. Still, the blue fire in his eyes was sending out a tangible heat that she could feel throughout her senses. Here comes the pass, she thought. Just be cool and calm. You can handle it.

But he threw her off balance a little by picking up another piece of the puzzle and inserting it into place. It fit snugly and perfectly, and Shelley's eyes followed the deliberate movement of his fingers with a curious fascination. Strong, working hands, she found herself thinking as she toyed with the little bit of an arching bridge in her palm. The hands of a man who had worked his way to success, not the hands of a man who'd had everything given to him on a silver platter.

"It fits," he noted quietly, reaching for another piece.

"Yes," she agreed faintly, forcing her eyes away from his fingers and searching out the right spot for her tiny portion of bridge. The iced-watermelon tint of her nails contrasted with the gray stone she was sliding into place. For some reason, it was a little difficult getting the piece to lock into position even though it was an obvious fit.

"Here, let me." The heavy, dark satin of Joel's voice was a barely murmured whisper as he gently took the puzzle piece from her fingers and pressed it into place with a tiny click. "It's an oddly satisfying feeling when the fit is perfect, isn't it?"

Her eyes flew instantly to meet his, seeking double meanings and innuendoes, but he merely smiled and picked up another piece. Still, she couldn't rid herself of the notion that there was an underlying sensuality in the way he had locked the bit of puzzle into place. It was her imagination, she thought nervously. Perhaps she shouldn't have any more of the cognac.

Taking a grip on her unwinding thoughts, she tugged them back into line and chose another section of bridge with a practiced eye. He watched for a moment as she deftly placed it, and then he slid the one he was holding in beside it, fitting the small tongue on his piece into the curved opening of hers. Again, the faint *frisson* of sensuality trickled along Shelley's nerves. Uneasily, she withdrew her fingers from the table and folded them in her lap as she searched for the next portion of the bridge.

Joel sipped his cognac and quietly toyed with a bit of water. When Shelley located another section of the stone bridge and settled it, he slipped his segment of water into the space just beneath the gracefully arching structure. Shelley's lashes fluttered briefly as she experienced a strange mental flash of standing on the stone bridge in the picture and staring down into the dark, mysterious depths of the water. Letting Joel make love to her would be every bit as dangerous as plunging headfirst off the bridge into the deep waters of the canal.

Now where the devil had that thought sprung from? She had absolutely no intention of letting Joel Cassidy carry her off to bed, and in all honesty, he showed no overt intention of even trying to do so! What was the matter with her this evening? One watermelon-colored nail tapped on the glass top of the table as she hunted for another section of puzzle.

Together they slowly built up the canal scene. A lingering silence hung over the room as the pattern took shape, and it wasn't only the pattern of the puzzle itself that was forming, Shelley was ultimately forced to realize. The pattern of the way Joel was playing the game was becoming just as obvious.

"Wouldn't you rather work on another section of the picture?" she finally asked tentatively as he once again waited until she had inserted a piece before he reached across to add one that fit snugly into hers.

"I wouldn't dream of trying to branch out on my own so early," he drawled softly. "I'll follow your lead for a while." He pressed the piece firmly into place, filling the groove that had been carved in the one she had found. Filling it completely.

Shelley tore her gaze away from the sight of his fingers moving with such sureness and care. Maybe what she needed was *more*, not less, of the cognac, she decided, lifting her glass.

"Joel?"

"Yes, Shelley?" He wasn't looking at her, his shimmering blue gaze following her fingers as she selected another piece.

"It's getting late. Was there anything else you wanted to discuss with me about our business agreement before you leave?" Yes, that was the right note to strike, she congratulated herself. Firm, with the beginnings of dismissal threading through her words. She snapped the segment of water into position with subtle decision. The time had come to send him home.

"No, there's nothing else we need to discuss concerning our business venture. Not tonight." With unerring accuracy, he had already located the segment of water that connected with the one she had placed.

Her fingertips were still hovering above the canal when he moved to slowly, deliberately insert his piece.

His hand brushed hers as he locked the bit of puzzle into place, and Shelley caught her breath as he abruptly snagged her fingers.

Her widening eyes met his across the table as he held her hand gently captive.

He smiled, a beguiling, infinitely promising, very masculine smile. "There's really nothing else to discuss, is there? When the fit is perfect, there is no need for words. Let me show you how well we go together, Shelley Banning."

Joel got to his feet in a slow-motion movement that drew her inevitably up beside him. This was it, Shelley told herself fleetingly. This was the seduction attempt she had been expecting. All she had to do was disengage herself and show him the door. All very polite, light, controlled.

But he was already sliding his hands along the black silk of her sleeve, and she could feel the faint roughness of his palms. The sensation was somehow different, compelling, binding. Before she could sort out the tingling impressions, he was folding her close, wrapping those strong, sure hands around her and forcing her gently against him, firmly into place.

Joel's mouth came down on hers even as he fitted her to his body, and the kiss, like his touch, held a strangely compelling quality. Shelley knew she should break it off and send him away, but a part of her insisted on sampling a little of the exploring, probing caress.

Her palms flattened against his shoulders, a small, steadying action meant to keep her from losing her balance. She would only stand here in the circle of his arms for a little while, Shelley promised herself. Just long enough to taste the promise in him.

"Shelley?"

Her name was a husky growl against her mouth, a male query to which he wanted only one reply. She would not give it. Instead, Shelley remained mute, and the lack of a verbal response seemed to provoke him into an escalation of the sensual assault. Joel's tongue began to probe the line of her lips, toying with the corner and then sliding wetly along their fullness to the opposite side. The strong fingers on her back found the sensitive base of her spine and pressed, urging her lower body into the cradle of his hips.

The intimate contact revealed his boldly rising desire, and the knowledge flashed in warning along her senses. But even as she tried to steady herself against his shoulders and make some effort to put a little distance between them, Joel's palms slid farther down, to the rounded curve of her derrière. She felt his fingers sink luxuriously into the shape of her, and the material of the white skirt provided minimal protection.

The audacious caress brought a moan to her lips. The sound was half a response and half a protest, but he wasted no time trying to analyze it.

"Oh!"

The instant her lips parted on the soft cry, he was seizing the opportunity, plunging deftly inside to find the warm dampness of her mouth. Shelley's eyes shut tightly against the reality of the passionate invasion. She didn't want to think about what all this meant, not yet. The palms with which she had tried to maintain her balance were moving softly on the material of his jacket now, seeking the shape of his shoulders. When his tongue found hers, the iced-watermelon nails curved abruptly into the fabric she had been smoothing.

As if that were the signal he had been waiting for, Joel moved, bending to lift her easily into his arms.

"Joel, no, I won't let you . . ." Her words were cut off as he closed her mouth once more with a kiss that he didn't break throughout the process of carrying her across the champagne-colored carpet to the deep-cordovan-brown couch.

Shelley knew a swirling sense of vertigo as he lowered himself to the cushions, settling her across his thighs. His lips never released hers.

Joel held the drugging kiss a moment longer, and then, with a hungry groan, he broke it off to begin a nuzzling exploration of her throat. Shelley gasped as his palm began simultaneously to glide over the curve of her hip and up toward the fullness of one breast.

"Shelley, I want you," he rasped against the exquisitely vulnerable skin just behind her ear.

"Joel, no," she protested weakly, compulsively turning her face into the safety of his chest. "It's—it's too soon, and we hardly know each other, and we're not"—she gulped for breath—"we're not exactly each other's type."

"None of that matters," he whispered. "Shelley, it can happen like this between two people. Let it happen to us. I've been wanting you all evening. I think I started wanting you when you walked into the shop this afternoon." He nipped persuasively at her earlobe, and she flinched.

"I know it can happen like that for a man," she mumbled. "But I'm just not interested in a one-night stand, Joel."

"Hardly that," he murmured, his tongue drawing erotic circles on the interior of her ear. "We're business partners now, remember?"

"There's an old and firm injunction against combining business with pleasure," she managed with a brave attempt at flippancy.

"So you admit there is some pleasure involved in this for you?" he asked, pouncing on her statement.

"Joel, don't you dare try to trick me into saying what

you want to hear!" She lifted her head for an instant, glaring up at him.

He raised his head to smile wistfully, hungrily down at her. "The key to winning the game is to learn all the tricks and patterns," he whispered.

When she opened her mouth to protest further, he sealed the words in her throat with his lips and in the same moment shifted the hand that had been lying in wait along her rib cage to cover her breast.

The deliberate, sure and possessive way he fitted the shape of her into his hand sent a tremor through Shelley's body. He drank the moan that rose in her throat, and then he began consolidating his advance against her senses by letting his fingers rasp the peak of her breast through the thin black silk and the lacy fabric of her bra.

"My God, woman!" he muttered a little shakily against her mouth, "do you know what it does to a man to get this kind of response from a woman he wants?"

"Joel . . ."

But she couldn't say anything else as the urgency rose in her body. She felt the tautening ache in her nipples and knew he was fully aware of it. As if he couldn't resist any longer, he began undoing the turquoise buttons of the black silk blouse with fingers that trembled slightly in passion.

He did want her, she thought dazedly. Whatever else she could say about Joel Cassidy, he was totally honest in his desire. There was an undeniable excitement and a deeply feminine satisfaction in that knowledge. When the black silk fell aside and he found the front clasp of her bra, she sighed against the skin of his throat, and her fingers slipped unconsciously inside his shirt. She began undoing buttons herself.

Gently, he forced her back into the cushions, moving to lower himself along the length of her as he tracked kisses down from the pulse point at the base of her throat to the rounded heaviness of her breasts.

Shelley sucked in her breath, and her fingers twined with sudden fierceness into the thick flame of his hair when he grazed the tight, hard nipples with his lips.

"Oh, Joel!" Her head arched back, and her lashes squeezed shut in reaction to the incredibly exciting touch of his mouth and his hands.

"The feel of you," he murmured huskily. "The hardness here—" he curled his tongue around the nipple— "and the softness here . . ." He kissed the full breast. "The feel of you could drive me insane this evening. Do you realize that?" His powerful hands moved down to grasp her hips as he closed his mouth back over first one rosy peak and then the other.

Then he shifted once more, urging her legs apart with his knee and making a place for himself between her thighs. Even though the material of their clothing remained between their bodies, the uncompromisingly intimate embrace was enough to take away Shelley's breath. In this position she was made fully aware of the state of his arousal, his hardness pressing against the softness of her with aggressive demand.

"Feel me, honey. Feel my need of you tonight . . ."

Joel's tongue surged between her lips, this time in a timeless pattern that was meant to invoke the image of another kind of joining.

"Joel!" Shelley cried his name softly when he ceased the plundering action for a moment to rain kisses across the ridge of her cheekbones.

"It's all right, my sweet little hustler. It's all right," he crooned. "We fit together like the pieces of your puzzle. It's all right."

It was the word "hustler" that finally managed to jangle the warning bells in her mind. It broke the spell that had begun binding her from the moment she had found herself seated across from Joel at the puzzle table, perhaps earlier. Damn it! She was not like him! She was not a *hustler!* She didn't take her pleasures where she found them or conclude a business deal with sex.

"Joel, that's enough," she got out tightly, beginning to push against his shoulders as her willpower returned. "That's far enough. Please!"

"Relax, honey. Relax and let me handle everything. It's going to be so good between us." He nipped passionately at the soft flesh of her shoulder as if gently punishing her for protesting.

"I said that's enough, Joel," she managed in a voice that was so steady she surprised herself with it. She didn't feel at all steady. Her body was still caught up in the sensuality of the moment even if her mind was recovering from the spell. "I meant it."

Something of her determination finally seemed to get through to him. With great reluctance, he raised his head to stare down into hazel eyes that were very deep and very green with the remnants of her arousal. But the flicker of decision swirled in those depths, too, and he saw it.

"Shelley, honey, don't do this to both of us. I want you, and I know you want me. Let it happen, sweetheart. Just let it happen," he begged hoarsely.

"No." She moved her head once in denial. "Joel, we have nothing but a business deal between us. That's not enough. I'm sorry I got carried away and let things go this far."

"Damn it, don't start apologizing for my seduction attempt," he grated. "When it's necessary, I'll do my own apologizing! But I don't think it's necessary this time," he added, rising slowly to a sitting position on the couch. The ice and diamonds of his eyes blazed hungrily down at her as he swept the disarray of her silk shirt and unfastened bra. "Unless, of course, I should apologize for not ignoring your protests and making love to you regardless. Would you rather I did that, Shelley? Take the decision out of your hands?"

"Don't be ridiculous," she whispered tightly, sitting up and quickly straightening her clothes. "You do your own apologizing, and I'll make my own decisions."

To her astonishment, he smiled, and his eyes softened as he watched her fumble with her clothing. "Fair enough. But I reserve the right to try to influence your decisions."

He got to his feet, reaching down to grasp her shoulders and lift her up beside him. Ignoring the wariness in her eyes, Joel bent and kissed her one more time, a slow, lingering kiss that said good night and promised a dangerous future.

"Take care, honey," he murmured, "and when you go to sleep tonight, remind yourself that you're involved in a business venture with someone who knows all the tricks and patterns of the game."

"Is that meant to be a warning?" she demanded briskly, feeling more secure now that she knew she at last had control over the evening.

He grinned, a slashing, piratical grin that somehow managed to menace and beguile at the same time. "You're a bright, up-and-coming type; you figure it out."

Joel turned and walked out the door without a backward glance.

3

Shelley gave the good news to Dean Ackerly late in the afternoon of the following day.

"You're kidding! You actually talked him into it?" The good-looking, slightly stocky man in front of her ran a hand through his light-brown hair and shook his head in amazement. "I can't believe it!"

Shelley eyed him wryly as she reached for some papers from the Ackerly file. "You don't have to look quite so stunned, Dean. I told you I was going to do what I could to help you save the firm, didn't I?"

"Yes, yes, of course," he said quickly, gray eyes rueful as he realized he'd shown something less than total confidence in her ability. "It's just that it was such a shot in the dark. I really didn't think he'd go for it. I was well aware that the loan was a favor to my father, not to me or to the firm. At the time, I don't think Cassidy even cared about collateral. Securing the money with Ackerly land was dad's idea, not his, I think. I'm not sure of all the details because I was living in California at the time, but I remember being shocked when I discovered dad had borrowed that kind of money from a man like Joel Cassidy. I was sure it would be the equivalent of getting involved with a professional loan shark! When I found out the money was interest-free and a favor to my father, I couldn't rid myself of the idea that there had to be a catch. Men like Joel Cassidy don't do that kind of favor!"

"The favor," Shelley pointed out coolly as she placed a financial spreadsheet on her desk, "was definitely to your father, not to you. From here on in, that loan is no longer interest-free. We're buying time, but time doesn't come cheap. Do you have any idea how much the interest amounts to on a hundred thousand dollars? He wants prime rate, by the way."

Dean winced a little but nodded. "If we can get the company back on its feet, we can handle that. Damn it, I should have returned a year ago. But I knew dad and I could never work together. The business was his, and we would have clashed from day one if I'd tried to help. He was as stubborn as—as I am," he concluded ruefully.

"We'll get things straightened out," Shelley assured him with a little more confidence than she actually felt. Part of pulling off a successful turnaround with a faltering company was instilling confidence in management that matters actually could be salvaged. The psychological side of business was as crucial as the financial side. It all fit together. Shelley winced at the memory those last words engendered. Was she fated to go through life equating the interlocking pieces of a puzzle to a game of seduction?

Dean was reaching into the briefcase he had brought

along, pulling out papers and notes, so he missed the
flash of unease in Shelley's features. By the time he had
straightened, she was once again all business, and together they went to work analyzing the assets, liabilities
and working capital of Ackerly Manufacturing.

They pored over the firm's records, searching out the
weakest areas and looking for ways to strengthen the
crucial, basic ones. It was nearly five o'clock when Dean
finally sat back with a sigh, rubbing his forehead.

"It's not going to be easy, is it?" he muttered dispirit-
edly.

"It can be done, Dean. That's the important thing. We
can keep the bank from panicking now that we can
concentrate on it and stop worrying about that Cassidy
loan. And if we play our cards right, we can avoid layoffs,
or at least long-term ones. The toughest part will be
learning to operate in a leaner, tighter way. Also, we've
got to sell off inventory and improve the cash flow as
quickly as possible. That means psyching up the market-
ing and sales people. Their attitude will be as crucial as
management's during this period."

He nodded. "That's my first priority on Monday
morning."

"Don't keep your employees in the dark. Let them
know everyone's involved in a team effort to salvage the
business and that you need their cooperation."

"Because I do." He smiled, getting to his feet.

"Yes, you do." She smiled back.

He looked at her. "Thanks, Shelley," he said quietly.
"When I talk to you, I get the feeling it can be done."

Shelley sensed the faint, new element of optimism in
the atmosphere and nodded quickly. "You'll make it
work, Dean."

He hesitated, and she knew he was about to say
something else when the buzzer of her intercom interrupted.

"Shelley, there's a Mr. Cassidy to see you." Carol Robinson's voice held a note of disapproval, and Shelley guessed immediately that the receptionist had been coerced into breaking in on the meeting. Knowing Joel, he had probably insisted she do so. "Shall I have him wait?" she added hopefully. Shelley heard the added word *indefinitely* tacked on silently. Carol would like nothing better than to tell her intimidator that Shelley was tied up and likely to remain so for some time. It sounded like an equally good idea to Shelley.

It was Dean who handled Shelley's moment of indecision. "This will be a good opportunity for me to tell him I appreciate what he's done for Ackerly," he said quickly, looking pleased. "Mind if I stick around and meet him?"

"No, no, of course not," she responded hurriedly. "Send him in, Carol. We're through with our meeting." She glanced up at Dean as she released the intercom switch. "There's, uh, no need to go overboard with your thanks, Dean," she tried to say swiftly. "I mean, he's doing you a favor, but it's not exactly a *free* favor and . . ."

The remainder of her words died on her lips as the door to the main office of Mason Wells & Associates opened and Joel Cassidy walked into the room. She had time to realize he was dressed in the blue jeans and cotton work shirt he'd worn the first time she'd met him and didn't look at all the part of a successful businessman before her attention was sidetracked by the almost tangible aura of challenge he brought with him into the office.

Dean, gentleman that he was, recovered from his surprise quickly, thrusting out his hand. "I'm Dean Ackerly, Mr. Cassidy, and I just want to say I really appreciate your cooperation in this matter. With Shelley's consulting help and financial expertise, we're going to put

Ackerly Manufacturing back on the right track. Don't worry about that loan. You'll get your money!"

"I know," Joel replied laconically, "with interest."

At least he didn't ignore Dean's outstretched hand, Shelley thought with relief. The handshake was exceedingly brief, but it did occur, together with a steel-eyed assessment of Dean Ackerly.

"Sorry to interrupt you, but I came to see Shelley about a business matter," Joel went on smoothly but very pointedly. "She's my accountant, too."

Dean arched one brow but responded to the dismissal politely. "That's quite all right, Mr. Cassidy. Shelley and I were finished for the day." He smiled engagingly at her. "I'll give you a call later about the current inventory levels, okay?"

"That'll be fine, Dean," she said tightly, annoyed not with him but with the other man. The door closed behind her client, and she whirled on Joel. "What in the world do you mean by telling him I'm your accountant? Do you always make up convenient lies when you want to get rid of someone? And what did you say to Carol to upset her? Under normal circumstances, she would never have interrupted me when she knew I had someone in my office!"

He ignored the controlled tirade, striding across the room to plant his large, square hands flat on the polished surface of her desk. "You never answered my question yesterday. Are you sleeping with him?"

"That's none of your damn business!"

"It sure as hell is. As his chief creditor outside the bank, I've got a right to know whether his accountant has a conflict of interests," Joel growled, his eyes raking her infuriated expression.

"Even if I am sleeping with him, there would be no conflict of interest, would there?" Shelley shot back with an acid sweetness. "Either way, I'd have Ackerly's best interests at heart!"

"If we're concerned with the *best interests* of everyone involved, I'd like to point out that it's definitely to your benefit to keep me in a good mood," he murmured with a soft menace that sent a shiver down Shelley's spine.

"Is this how you intimidated poor Carol? Did you lean over her desk and threaten her?" she countered.

"Who the hell is this Carol person you keep worrying about?" But he straightened away from her desk and began pacing around the small room, examining the functional furniture, the plants she had hung in the window and the stack of professional magazines. He reminded her of a panther in a cage. The restless power combined with his obvious irritation to produce an intimidating effect.

"Carol is the receptionist you pressured into interrupting my meeting with Dean."

"Oh, her." He clearly lost interest in Carol. "I just told her I wanted to see you. Now." He paused by the window to stare out at the high-rise building across the street. "Are you sleeping with him, Shelley?" This time the question was a gentle, wistful request. Shelley didn't trust the tone for a minute.

"Why are you here, Joel?" she asked with a sigh.

"To talk you into having dinner with me again tonight," he admitted, swinging around to pin her with that perceptive gaze. Then he glanced at the thin gold watch on his wrist. "You're about through for the day, aren't you? I know a great little Mexican place where they make their own tortillas and green corn tamales."

Shelley jumped at the first excuse she could think of. "Thanks, but last night blew my diet for a month. Besides, I've got some work to do at home and I—"

"And you don't want to listen to me ask about your

relationship with Ackerly all evening," he concluded for
her, nodding in resignation. "Okay, you have my word. I
won't ask you again if you're sleeping with him, all right?
Look, you have to eat something, Shelley. Come out
with me and have a quick bite. I want to talk to you." Joel
gave her an appealing glance, shoving the fingers of one
large hand distractedly through the red depths of his hair.

Shelley knew she ought to refuse, knew he was
manipulating her, but for some reason she found herself
surrendering to the persuasive request she saw in his
eyes. She hesitated a moment longer and then gave in
completely. "I'll go out with you for a bite, Joel, if you
promise to take me some place that has a salad bar," she
finally managed with a wary smile. "And provided that
you really do have some honest business to discuss with
me!"

"Oh, I have business to discuss, all right," he said,
grinning. "I told Ackerly the truth. You're my new
accountant!"

Shelley paused in the act of refiling some Ackerly
Manufacturing paper work into her desk drawer. "What's
that supposed to mean?" she asked suspiciously.

"It means I'm dumping my present staid, conservative
firm in favor of someone more in tune with my own way
of doing business," he said glibly.

"Who is your present firm?" When he told her, she
raised one eyebrow. "They're one of the 'Big Eight,'
Joel. Why in the world would you want to get rid of
them?"

"I chose the firm because I figured it would help to
have one of the top multinational accounting firms listed
on my income tax return as the preparer. Didn't help,"
he added with a philosophical shrug. "I got audited,
anyway!"

"They sent someone to defend you at the IRS audit,
didn't they?"

"Sure, and they cleared everything with the Internal Revenue Service. I won the audit, but it cost me a fortune, and it proved having a big, expensive accounting firm's name on my tax return wasn't going to keep the IRS from scrutinizing it. So when you showed up in my life, I decided I might as well start working with an accountant who knows how to hustle. Someone," he went on blandly, "who, because she needs some big accounts to get started when she goes into business for herself, will give me the attention I need and deserve. Between saving Ackerly Manufacturing and having a client like me, you'll be in great shape to open your own firm."

Shelley stared at him. "You're serious, aren't you?"

"I never say anything I don't mean. Ready to go?" He glanced at her cleared desk.

"Joel, wait a minute. You can't just walk in here and announce you're going to be one of my new clients," she gasped as the full implications of the statement dawned.

"Why not?" He looked genuinely curious.

"Because—because that sort of decision needs to be carefully thought out and carefully analyzed. You know nothing about my skills. You're currently with one of the biggest accounting firms in the nation and—"

"Bigger is not necessarily better in the accounting business, Shelley," he noted gently. "There are a lot of other factors to be considered, not the least of which is getting an accountant who understands me. It's rather like choosing a wife, you see."

"How many wives have you chosen using this technique?" she snapped before she could stop herself.

"None yet," he retorted easily, "but if the technique works when choosing an accountant, I may give it a try in other areas."

Shelley scrabbled for the silver-studded turquoise shoulder bag that she had worn with her white business suit, deliberately not meeting his mocking gaze. He took her arm as she came a bit reluctantly from behind the desk, and a moment later they were walking through the darkened outer office. Everyone else had already left for the day, apparently.

He was absolutely right, Shelley thought as Joel handed her into the waiting Maserati. She might find him annoying on occasion and perhaps not quite what she would wish in the line of business partners, but having him for a client would be a major coup. An excellent way to start off a new firm, she reflected. His account, combined with the reputation for having salvaged Ackerly Manufacturing, would almost assure her success. She was mentally considering the potential brightness of her future when they cruised past her car in the parking lot.

"Joel, wait a minute. What about my car?"

"We can pick it up after dinner," he told her, pulling out into the busy afternoon traffic before she could think of an argument.

"Well, all right, I suppose that will work," she agreed tentatively, her mind still spinning with his earlier announcement. "Joel, are you serious about this business of switching accountants?" She turned in the seat to address his profile.

"Yes." He didn't take his eyes off the flow of traffic, but he accompanied the affirmative with a nod. "We can talk about it over dinner."

A sudden thought made her chew her lip anxiously for an instant before Shelley said very carefully, "I consider myself fairly *aggressive* when it comes to accounting practices, Joel, but I'm not—" She hesitated, searching for the right word. "I'm willing to go into the so-called gray areas when filing an income tax return, but I . . ." Her second attempt to clarify her role dissolved.

He threw her a flashing grin, his eyes laughing at her.

"But you're straight, right? You wouldn't help a client, even a good one, break the law."

"That's about it," she said quietly.

"You think I'd ask you to do that?" He sounded more curious than upset.

"Would you?" There was no sense skirting the issue, Shelley thought grimly. They might as well know where they stood with each other right from the beginning.

"Relax. I'm aggressive, too, but I do want to stay in business! I won't be demanding anything unprofessional from you in the way of accounting practices. Satisfied?"

"I only wanted to make certain we understood each other." She smiled in relief.

"I understand you perfectly," he drawled. "And I think the reverse is true, too, although it may take you a while to admit it."

"No cryptic remarks before dinner," she warned him grimly.

"Speaking of which, here we are. Are you sure you just want a salad?"

"No fair tempting your accountant." Shelley eyed the little restaurant and inwardly stifled a groan. She loved Mexican food.

He sighed. "Do you always make so many rules?"

"No questioning your accountant's rules or the number thereof. She knows what's best."

"I can see we're going to have a lot of fun together," he muttered, parking the car in the tiny lot behind the restaurant.

Shelley never had a chance to inquire about a salad bar. Joel had taken the precaution of phoning in an order for both of them, and when the enthusiastic staff greeted him like an old friend and began producing homemade tortilla chips with two kinds of hot sauces, the fabulous tamales and several other specialties, Shelley gave up the battle.

"I'll get even for this," she vowed at one point, tasting her margarita with undisguised appreciation.

"Now who's resorting to threats?" he complained, downing a taco in a few man-sized gulps.

The rest of the meal passed in a pleasant haze of tart margaritas and spicy food. The conversation was surprisingly easygoing for two people who were practically strangers, Shelley thought at one point. But perhaps that was the advantage of having a business association. It gave two people the feeling they knew more about each other than was actually the case.

"Do you realize we haven't actually discussed your amusement-company business or your real estate wheeling and dealing?" she finally observed as the dinner drew to a close. "This was supposed to be a business meal!"

"We'll get down to business after we finish," he responded, blue eyes gleaming.

"If you're talking about another seduction attempt, I can tell you right now you'll be wasting your time!" Shelley made a show of collecting her purse as Joel asked for the check.

"I would never equate business with seduction," he told her, contriving to appear hurt by the accusation. "I said we'd get down to business, and I meant it. Come on."

He grabbed her wrist and led her out the door as the staff bid them a cheerful good-by. But when they reached the street, Joel didn't guide her toward the little parking lot at the rear; instead, he started briskly down the sidewalk.

"Where are we going? And wherever it might be, you'll have to slow down. I'm wearing heels."

"Sorry." He obediently slowed his long, ground-eating stride and released her hand to put his arm comfortably around her waist. "We're almost there."

"Where?" She glanced around the street, which was rapidly being enshrouded by night. Most of the businesses were closed for the evening, but a few small restaurants and taverns were still open.

"The shopping mall in the next block," he explained, drawing to a halt to wait patiently for the light at the crosswalk.

"The shopping mall!"

"I want to show you something."

He was obviously not going to enlighten her further. The mall in the next block contained a couple of department stores, several little shops and some restaurants, all of which were still open. A large number of people were thronging the wide, central corridor of the indoor mall, window-shopping or waiting for someone. Shelley had shopped there frequently, and she knew the stores well. She couldn't imagine why Joel had brought her there that evening, though.

"I'm going to put my foot down very firmly if you're thinking of taking me to the ice cream parlor," she told him as they started down the interior of the mall, which had been designed to resemble a Mexican plaza.

"We can talk about ice cream later. Don't be so greedy. I've fed you enough for one evening."

And then she saw where he was taking her, and a slow, rueful smile lit her eyes. "Don't tell me; let me guess. Not content with corrupting my diet, you're going to try to undermine my high moral standards!"

The arcade was undoubtedly the single busiest location in the mall. It was obviously the place the kids headed for while their mothers went shopping, and it had probably done more to halt the whining of ten-year-olds than any other single invention in the twentieth century. No longer did they have to submit to being dragged through lingerie departments or long aisles of housewares. Mom could take her own sweet time browsing, secure in the knowledge that she knew exactly where to locate her offspring when the time came to leave.

Bright lights dazzled the eye, sophisticated computer graphics flashed across rows of video screens and an incredible cacophony of sounds emanated from the simulated flight decks of starships and missile command centers. The young video-game players seemed blessed with an endless stream of quarters, which they plunked into the machines with the same abandon that adults pulled slot-machine handles in Las Vegas.

"Your moral standards I will attend to on my own," Joel promised, guiding her into the darkened arcade. It was difficult plowing a path through the ranks of kids competing eagerly for machines. "This is business." He gestured with a sweeping hand. "And this," he added politely as a man emerged from the back of the room, "is Rick Bradley, the man responsible for keeping all these young hoodlums in line. Rick, this is Shelley Banning."

"And for keeping them in change, too, I gather," Shelley said with a smile, putting out her hand to the young, tawny-haired man wearing a canvas change apron around his narrow waist.

Rick rustled the quarters in his apron and grinned good-naturedly. "Wouldn't want any of these young folk to miss out on the fun just because they didn't have change for a dollar." A faint southern accent underlined his words.

"I'm sure their parents are most appreciative," Shelley mocked, glancing at the rows of avid players.

"Nothing comes free in life," Joel told her, "not even a mechanical baby sitter. In any event, I figure I'm contributing to the kids' education."

"Teaching them how to defend the planet earth against attacks by alien beings?" she asked, watching one youngster madly manipulating a control panel in an attempt to ward off just such an encounter.

"No, no, no," Joel chided, leading her over to watch the game from behind the boy's shoulder. "You miss the point. These games develop split second decision making and judgment. And just look at the demands it makes on eye-hand coordination."

"No doubt about it," Shelley agreed soberly. "He will emerge from this arcade a much sharper, more coordinated kid, able to make rapid-fire decisions and return a tennis serve with skill and precision."

"And there is the added benefit that he will be able to defend earth in the event of alien attack," Joel concluded.

Shelley laughed, shaking her head in surrender. "What can I say? You're clearly an unsung hero in the cause of American education."

"You can always find something nice to say about everyone if you try." Joel leaned forward and tapped the kid on the shoulder as the game came to an end with the simulated roar of an exploding rocket and a brilliant display of computerized fireworks. "Which game do you like better? This one or the new one over in the corner?" he asked interestedly.

The boy glanced up at him with questioning blue eyes. "I like the new one best, but this one's okay. There's too long a line at the other one." He turned back to his machine, fishing another quarter out of his pocket. "And I still have a lot to learn about this one. I've never gotten beyond the third level." There was blatant speculation in the boy's expression as he innocently asked, "Did you want to play?"

"Well, I was thinking of showing my accountant here how it works," Joel said, smiling benignly down at the boy.

"I hate to give it up because it's tough to find another game open right now," the young man said slowly, his light-brown hair a casual mop around his head as he looked at the crowded room. "But we could, uh, take turns." There was now a definitely hopeful gleam in the boy's eyes as he gazed upward at the redheaded stranger. He rattled the quarters in his pocket suggestively.

"Never got beyond the third level, huh?" Joel shoved his hands into the back pocket of his jeans and eyed the video game reflectively.

"No, sir. It's a hard game," the boy assured him earnestly.

"Tricky, hmmm?"

"Yes, sir. Want to play?"

"What's your name, kid?"

"Steve. I'm ten."

"Okay, Steve, my name's Joel. And I appreciate your offer to take turns."

"I was thinking," Steve began cautiously, "we could sort of, well, compare scores when we got done, you know?"

Shelley stifled a burst of laughter at the obvious ploy, but her eyes danced as Joel frowned consideringly and appeared to mull the idea over in his mind. She waited expectantly for him to decline the contest.

"Compare scores, hmm?"

"Yeah, you know, see who gets the highest." Steve nodded eagerly.

"And what does the high scorer get?" Joel persisted.

"How about a free game paid for by the one with the lower score?" Somehow Steve managed to make the idea sound ingenuous. He rattled the quarters in his pocket again. "My mom won't be back for me for another hour."

"You're on, kid. You go first."

"Joel!" Shelley's disapproval showed in her voice. "Surely you're not going to—to *bet* with this child on the outcome of a game!"

Joel and Steve both turned to stare at her as if she were one of the alien invaders against whom they would be defending the planet.

"Who did you say this was?" Steve asked with a frown.

"My accountant," Joel explained as they both turned back to the machine.

"Is that like a girl friend?" Steve put his quarter into the slot.

"Yeah."

Shelley muttered something vindictive that went unheard amid the various explosions and other audio feedback coming from the video games in the arcade. It wouldn't have mattered if she'd raised the level of her voice, however. Neither Joel nor Steve was showing any inclination to listen. Their total concentration was focused on the space war game being played out on the screen. If Steve paid half as much attention to his school work, he would probably graduate at the head of his class, Shelley decided, and in the same moment told herself it was highly unlikely the boy showed quite the same level of concentration in the classroom. It was highly doubtful any of the avid players did. Pity. A lot of talent waiting to be tapped.

The game progressed fast and furiously as one alien invader after another was obliterated. Steve racked up a high score before losing his last defender and turned the machine over to Joel with an anticipatory smirk. Joel dropped a quarter into the slot and went to work.

He was good, but not quite good enough. The alien invaders went down quickly, but not quite as quickly as they had when Steve had been in command of the console. In the end, it was the ten-year-old's score that stood highest, and Joel admitted defeat with good grace.

"Thanks for the game, Steve. I'll see you around." He shoved the payoff quarter into the slot, and the grinning kid went happily back to playing his free game.

"Serves you right to lose after falling for such an obvious hustle," Shelley muttered as Joel took her arm and guided her toward the arcade entrance.

"I'm a sucker for fast cons." He sighed, his gaze swinging rapidly around the arcade as they left. "You should know."

"Joel!"

"It looks like I'll have to get some more machines like that one in the corner. The one Steve said he preferred. Look how the kids are lined up for it. That's the trouble with this business now that the pinballs have been superseded by these new video games. There's much more of a demand for the latest machine on the market. I'm having to replace the games far more quickly as they go out of favor. It was different with pinball. One pinball game stayed popular almost indefinitely."

"You sound so wistful!" she teased.

"There are compensations with the new machines," he admitted. "Every game is a paid game. They're not designed to reward the player with free plays the way the old pinballs were. You can extend a video game, but you can't win a free one the way you could on a classic pinball machine."

"Looks like your friend Steve has found a way to get himself an occasional free game," Shelley observed wryly as they stepped out into the mall. "Imagine learning that sort of behavior at his age! And you contributed to it!"

"For some of us it comes naturally, I suppose," he said, grinning.

"If you accuse me of being a hustler one more time, you'll find yourself looking for another accountant," she vowed, lifting her chin.

"Don't worry, I'm learning when to keep my mouth shut."

She threw him an uneasy, faintly suspicious glance, but he returned it with a charming smile that set her pulse racing. What in the world is wrong with me, she thought wonderingly. I have no business finding myself attracted to a man like this. And that was what was happening, she realized with sudden apprehension. She was attracted to this man, and that seemed abruptly a very dangerous situation in which to find herself. There were sound, logical reasons why people warned against mixing business with pleasure.

But the evening had been fun, and Shelley had enjoyed herself more than she had for a long time. The temptation to forget that this man was a business associate and a rather threatening one at that was strong.

She was dwelling on such thoughts as Joel helped her into the car and slid in beside her, filling the leather cockpit with his easy power and grace.

For a time, silence hovered in the intimate confines of the Maserati as Joel sent it back out into traffic. Shelley's mind continued to spin with the realization of her own awareness of the man beside her and the warnings she tried to issue to herself. Several minutes passed before she awoke to the fact that they weren't headed back to her office parking lot.

"Joel? My car," she began uncertainly. "You'll have to take me back to the office."

"I'm taking you home first," he said simply. "My home."

Shelley swallowed tensely. "I don't think that's a very good idea," she tried to say steadily. She had to remain firm and in command, she reminded herself. Firm and in command.

"I think it's an excellent idea," he countered lightly. "Didn't you hear me tell Steve that accountants were a little like girl friends?"

4

Just one nightcap, Shelley," Joel went on persuasively as she sat mute in her corner of the seat. "I want to show you my home. You've seen something of the business side of my life; now I want you to see the other side."

Shelley considered that, knowing she was tempted. A part of her was deeply curious to see Joel Cassidy in his home setting. "All right, one drink, Joel, and then I must be on my way. Do you understand?" She glanced at him with an anxiety she hoped was concealed. Going home with Joel Cassidy was not the smartest move she could be making, and Shelley was honest enough to admit it to herself.

"I understand." He flicked her a satisfied smile and then returned his attention to the road.

It wouldn't have mattered, Shelley realized, what answer she had given him. He had already made the decision to take her home, and it wasn't likely she could have changed it. But she could handle the situation, she told herself firmly. She would have the drink and then insist he take her back to where she had left her car.

That decision made, it became much easier to relax in the white leather seat. She had sent Joel Cassidy home on his own last night, and she could deal with a repeat performance, if necessary, tonight. Was she overconfident? Shelley didn't think so. She knew her own capabilities.

"What are you thinking about over there in the moonlight?" Joel asked softly.

"Capabilities."

"Your own or mine?" He chuckled.

"Mine."

"If you're worried about whether or not you can handle the accounting for my business—" he began firmly.

"I'm not."

He grinned knowingly. "You don't lack self-confidence, do you?"

She thought about that seriously for a moment. "I know the extent of my skills, and I know in which direction I want my career to go. The rest is just a lot of hard work, isn't it?"

"And a few lucky breaks," he agreed.

"Like having you walk into my office and toss your business into my lap," she admitted, smiling. "Or inheriting the Ackerly account."

"Everyone gets a few lucky breaks. What counts is having the courage to use them."

"Are you speaking from experience?"

"Of course. Look how I'm taking advantage of the lucky break you gave me when you walked into my shop yesterday. There I was, thinking how badly I needed a new accountant, and suddenly you appeared!"

"And the first thing I did was talk you out of the use of a hundred thousand dollars. Not everyone would see that as a lucky break, Joel." But she was laughing silently in the shadows.

"Not everyone has the skill and experience to look beneath the surface of a situation. And besides, even lucky breaks don't come free in this world." The tone of his voice suddenly changed, becoming more aloof. "What did you think of the arcade tonight?"

Shelley lifted one shoulder vaguely. "It looked profitable, and it looked like the kids were having fun. I'll reserve judgment on the issue of how much you're contributing toward American education."

"All the machines aren't in such innocuous surroundings, you realize," he went on deliberately. "A lot are in bars and pool halls and bowling alleys."

"As your accountant, I won't have to visit every location, surely?" she murmured.

"No."

"What are you getting at, Joel?"

He was silent for a moment, and then he said quietly, "I make a lot of money, Shelley, but I don't belong to a country club, and I'm not called on to put on a black tie for social charity functions, and I spend a lot of time in those bars, pool halls and bowling alleys. I can offer you money but not a lot of social status."

She went very still. What was he trying to say? "But as your accountant, it's only your money I'm interested in, isn't it?" she finally managed flippantly.

He laughed abruptly and murmured something she didn't quite catch.

"What was that?" she demanded, eyes narrowing.

"I said you were a hustler after my own heart."

"I thought you were learning when to keep your mouth shut!"

"It takes practice."

It was too late to insist he turn the car around and take
her back to the office, Shelley told herself. She didn't
want to be too rude to a man she needed so much.
Needed in a business sense, that was. And she had
enjoyed herself this evening.

When he eventually parked the white Maserati in the
circular drive of a home surrounded by the natural desert
setting of an expensive residential area, Shelley found
herself suddenly eager to see the interior. Her curiosity
about Joel Cassidy was unusual. She generally didn't
care much about a client's personal life; only his or her
financial situation. But with Joel things were different.
Dangerously different.

"It's lovely," she said sincerely as he walked her to the
front door of the sleek, contemporary home. It was white
with a red tile roof and surrounded by a deliciously cool
garden.

"Thanks," he nodded, obviously pleased. "I bought it
a year ago. I'm glad you like it."

As soon as she stepped inside, Shelley realized that the
focal point of the house was the large private patio that
swept the length of the structure. Wall-to-wall green-
house windows took full advantage of the view of lush
garden and sparkling, underwater-lit pool. It was difficult
to tell where the outdoors ended and the interior of the
house began.

Polished wooden steps marked an inviting array of
levels inside, leading down to a two-story living room and
up to a circular kitchen and dining area, all opening out
onto the patio.

The rooms were furnished in cool woods, light natural
shades that were well suited to the desert style of living,
and here and there was a touch of unexpected drama,
such as the gleaming stainless-steel fireplace.

Automatically, Shelley went toward the wall of glass,

drawn by the dramatically lit garden and pool on the
other side. Behind her she heard Joel go into the kitchen
and open a cabinet. "The place is beautifully designed,"
she said, turning as she heard him come back down into
the living room. "Do you swim a lot?" She almost winced
at the trite question. Somehow it was difficult to summon
up the lighthearted banter she knew would be more
appropriate to the situation.

"Almost daily." He smiled, handing her a stemmed
glass filled with a dark coffee-flavored liqueur topped with
thick cream. "Do you?" The blue eyes flared softly.

"Oh, yes, whenever I get the chance," she said
hurriedly, wondering why the conversation, which had
been so easy and casual all evening, was now threatening
to disintegrate. She turned back toward the window,
sipping the potent liqueur through the layer of cream.
Joel came to stand close behind her.

"Do you want to swim tonight?" he asked gently.

Her head came up swiftly as she glanced back at him.
"Not unless you happen to keep a closetful of women's
swim suits handy for visitors!" she told him a bit tartly.

"You'd insist on a suit?" he sighed.

"I'm afraid so."

"I could loan you one of mine," he said, grinning.

"Thanks, but no thanks." She smiled, relaxing under
the warmth of his humor. That slightly crooked tooth was
a most endearing touch in his hard, bluntly carved face,
she thought fleetingly. And the steel in those eyes wasn't
a cold metal at all. Instead, it seemed to provide a
platinum warmth that could ensnare a woman who
wasn't exceedingly cautious.

"Let's go out and sit beside the pool to finish drinking
these." Joel slid aside a wide glass door and ushered her
out onto the patio. He settled her into a padded lounger
and seated himself in the one beside her. For a long

moment they sipped their drinks and stared at the pool in companionable silence. The play of shadow and light on the underwater-lit surface was as intriguing as the flames of a fireplace. In the soft darkness it was possible to relax completely, and Shelley felt herself slipping under the spell of the moment.

As she realized what was happening, Shelley paused mentally to hover on some invisible brink. It was suddenly important to make something very clear to Joel Cassidy.

"Joel?"

"Hmmm?" His eyes met hers with a steady warmth.

"What you said about an accountant being somewhat like a—a girl friend . . ."

He smiled but said nothing, and she went on cautiously, tearing her eyes away from his. "I don't make a very good girl friend, Joel."

"Girl friend isn't quite the right word," he murmured, lifting a finger to trace the line of her jaw. "It's a ten-year-old kid's word. My word, the right word, would be a little different. Lover, perhaps."

Shelley's fingers tightened on the stem of her glass, and she said, her voice raw, "I don't make a very good lover, either, Joel." She stared fiercely at the shimmering surface of the pool, waiting.

"What are you trying to tell me?" he whispered, his fingers sliding from her jaw to the nape of her neck, where they played coaxingly just beneath the curve of her hair.

"I was married for a year, and it wound up in disaster. I've been engaged once since then, and the relationship fell apart before we got to the altar. I've dated frequently, and none of my dating relationships have ever lasted very long." Her grip on the glass grew tighter. Why was she telling him all this? It was none of his business, and the subject was far too intimate. But she couldn't seem to stop herself, and the excitingly roughened fingertips at the nape of her neck never ceased their persuasive, subtle seduction.

"Meaning?"

"Meaning I'm willing to have dinner with you occasionally and willing to do business with you. But I'm not willing to be a temporary lover for you," she said quietly. "If that's really what you're looking for in an accountant, you'd better look elsewhere."

He ignored that. "What went wrong in your marriage?"

She bit her lip, uncertain what to do, now that she'd opened up the subject. It was easiest to answer the question. "We were classmates in college. Carl always knew exactly where he was going and what he wanted out of life. I admired that. He was hired into a large corporation, and it was clear from the beginning that he was on a fast-track promotion program. Destined for success," she added with a hint of bitterness, pausing to sip the drink in her hand. "But it soon became obvious that one of the things he wanted out of life was a corporate wife. Someone who would devote her life to his career and could handle the entertaining, the social functions, the horrible hours, the lack of attention, all without a complaint. I started complaining almost at once. I wanted my own career, and while I was willing to assist in his, I wasn't willing to give up everything for it. Carl was a man who could make decisions quickly and act just as fast. When it became clear I wasn't going to shape up as a suitable corporate wife, he divorced me before I could become a liability."

"And the broken engagement which came later?" Joel prompted, apparently unperturbed.

"I broke it off because I realized that I was once again

getting involved with the wrong kind of man. It wasn't fair to him, and I knew it would only wind up in the divorce courts again. I couldn't stand the thought!"

"What was wrong about him?"

"He was a lot like Carl. Ambitious, successful, motivated. I can't seem to help admiring those qualities in a man, yet they always conflict with what I seem to need," she whispered helplessly, not understanding it herself.

"You mean that even though the men you choose have those qualities themselves, they don't seem to understand and accept such traits in you, right?" Joel asked with a perception that brought Shelley's head around sharply. She peered at him through the shadows.

"Maybe that's it," she admitted, shaking her head once in frustration. "I can have a business relationship with the kind of man I admire, and I can even have a very casual dating relationship. But whenever things start becoming more involved and I start looking for understanding and acceptance from such a man, it all falls apart."

Joel leaned closer, the fingers at her nape clasping her gently now and holding her still. "The problem is that you just didn't meet the right man until you met me, Shelley Banning. I understand and accept you completely because you're a lot like me. I see nothing wrong in making love to a business partner or in doing business with a lover."

The last word was breathed against her mouth, and in the next instant his lips closed beguilingly over hers. She knew she should be protesting that his attitude was all mixed up, that there *was* something wrong in making love to a business partner, but Shelley couldn't find the will to summon up the argument. With a shudder, she relaxed languidly beneath the kiss.

It was slow and delicious, damp and invading, and she realized she'd had Joel's kiss in her head since the night before. It had nibbled around the edge of her consciousness, sometimes reminding her of its presence forcefully, other times receding patiently into the background, but always there. Always there. And tonight it was there in reality once more.

"Shelley," he growled achingly against her mouth as he pulled her to her feet. "I've been thinking about last night all day. Do you understand? I've been wanting you all day. When I got to your office this afternoon and found you closeted with Ackerly, I could cheerfully have throttled you!"

"He's my client," she protested.

"So am I. Do you kiss him the way you kiss me? Does your mouth open for him the way it does for me? Do your breasts fill his hands the way they fill mine?"

"Joel, stop it!" she begged, crowding closer beseechingly. His hands had moved to cup the soft swell of her breasts as he'd grated the question against her mouth. "I don't want to talk about Dean Ackerly."

"Neither do I."

He shut off further conversation by thrusting his tongue aggressively between her lips, hunting a response as his fingers slipped the white suit jacket from her shoulders and dropped it soundlessly onto the lounger. When she stirred with a strange restlessness, he stilled her movements by finding the shape of her rounded bottom and guiding her close against the outline of his body.

Shelley thrilled to the taut, waiting hardness of him. The scent of him filled her nostrils, musky and clean and all male. Unthinkingly, she began toying with the buttons of his shirt and finally undid them slowly, shakily.

He was with her all the way, and she closed her eyes as he undid the turquoise silk blouse and found the clasp of her bra. Shelley moaned softly into his shoulder as he removed the blouse and the lacy undergarment. He was nipping seductively at the line of her throat now, and his teeth tantalized her unbearably as his thumbs moved raspingly across her budding nipples.

"I need the softness of you tonight," Joel muttered thickly. "I need to make you mine. Give yourself to me, sweetheart."

"Joel, I can't think. I don't know what I want," she confessed bemusedly, aware that the folds of the snare were closing in around her.

"Yes, you do. Your body knows what it wants." His palms grazed the tips of her breasts, coaxing forth the response she could not hide. "Don't try to analyze this, honey. Just let go and trust me."

Trust? What a strange word for him to use, she thought vaguely. But her fingertips had discovered the curling auburn hair on his chest and began tracing tiny circles around the male nipples. When he caught his breath and sucked in his taut stomach, Shelley knew an exhilarating sense of power and longing that washed out other, more cautious emotions completely.

Her skirt slipped to the ground, forming a pool of white at her feet. When she stood before him wearing only her panties, Joel ran his hands lingeringly down the curves of her breasts, the contour of her waist and the fullness of her thighs. He groaned passionately into the hollow of her shoulder.

"Finish undressing me, honey. Touch me all over. I want to go crazy under your hands tonight."

Trembling with the force of her excitement and growing need, Shelley fumbled with the elaborate western buckle of his jeans and then slid down the zipper. In a moment, he was as naked as she, wearing only his close-fitting briefs.

The evidence of his arousal was bold and blatant beneath the thin cotton of his underwear, and Shelley gasped a little as he pressed himself close once more. Her nails bit into the skin of his shoulder as he slid his hips against hers with masculine demand.

At the sound of her half-stifled moan, Joel stooped and lifted her high into his arms, finding her mouth once more with his own and holding it captive as he strode to the end of the pool.

"Joel?" she got out questioningly as he started down the steps into the water.

"I invited you to go swimming, remember?" He lifted his head to study her with a lambent gaze.

"I remember." She could feel the flames from his eyes as they licked across her body, and then the sensation became confused with the cool lap of water against her warm skin. Shelley felt caught and suspended between the flames and the water, and she hovered, entranced in an exquisite torment of her senses.

He held her to him as he waded out into deeper water. When he came to a halt, the glistening blue water was up to his shoulders, and Shelley was floating in it, anchored by his arms. Slowly, he eased himself backward until he was treading water with long sweeps of his legs. When she wound her arms around his neck, he released her to use his own to keep them both afloat.

"You have to hold on tightly or you might go under," he advised with sensual amusement in his expression.

"I'll hold on tightly," she promised.

"On the other hand, going under might not be so bad."

"You think not?"

"Not as long as I'm there with you." He floated them backward toward the edge of the pool, his glowing gaze going to the softness of her breasts as they were crushed wetly against his chest.

When he reached the side of the pool, Joel once more stood erect, but when Shelley automatically started to slide her hands down from behind his neck, he caught her wrists and pressed them back into position.

She sighed achingly as he kissed her deeply, and then she felt his hands on the wisp of her panties, sliding them off until they were gone completely.

"Oh, Joel."

He sipped his name from her mouth while he began to probe the lower regions of her body, searching out the feminine secrets there. With one arm wrapped snugly around her back, he tangled his fingers in the toast-colored thicket between her legs.

Shelley stiffened momentarily at the blatant invasion, but he whispered and caressed until she relaxed against him. Deftly, he pulled her closer in the water, inserting his hair-roughened thigh between hers and gently forcing her body to open further to his touch.

"Trust me, honey," he breathed huskily into her ear as she buried her face in his shoulder. "I know you. I understand you. It's going to be all right."

She wanted to believe him; indeed, in the intoxicating depths of his spell, it was impossible not to believe him. A part of her whispered warnings against the seduction, but she thrust them aside, preferring instead to luxuriate in the feel of his hard, water-slicked body. She nuzzled his throat and slipped her hands inside the elastic waistband of his briefs.

"Yes, sweetheart, yes, *please*," he encouraged hoarsely.

Shelley shivered as he stroked the heart of her desire, learning the contours of her body thoroughly and sending ripples of pleasure through her as he did so.

"Oh!"

The throaty cry was a gasp from her lips as she let herself take the thrilling excitement he was offering, and her flattened palms pushed downward, removing the

briefs he wore. She felt the fullness of his arousal as she
dared to touch him as intimately as he was touching her.

"My God! Tonight you hold me in the palm of your
sweet hand in more ways than one, Shelley, honey. I
think it would leave me aching for a month if you were to
refuse me what I need so desperately this evening!" The
words were raw and a little savage, and he ended the
statement by grasping her hips and lifting her several
inches in the water. When her breasts emerged above the
surface, he lowered his head and tasted the hard buds of
her nipples.

Shelley balanced herself with her hands on his shoulders, breathing deeply as she reacted to the passionate
hold he had on her. When he lowered her gently again,
her mind was whirling and cloudy with desire, and she
whispered his name over and over as he toyed with the
wetness of her lips.

"Sweetheart," he murmured urgently in between the
hungry, biting kisses. "Honey, listen to me. Can I make
love to you now? Are you protected?"

For a moment, she couldn't understand what he
meant, and then she realized exactly what he was asking
and shook her head dazedly, eyes opening wide and
appealing.

"No! Oh, no. Joel, I'm sorry, I'm not—I mean there
hasn't been any reason—that is I haven't been—"

"Hush," he growled, silencing the stammering flow of
feminine apology. She thought she detected a thread of
satisfied humor in him. "Can I take it from that rather
unstructured sentence that you're not currently sleeping
with Dean Ackerly or anyone else?"

"You're a brute. You know that, don't you?" she
groaned accusingly. "No, there is no one else."

"Good," he said in a dragon's purr of masculine
content. "Then that leaves only me, doesn't it?"

"What would you have done if I'd told you there was someone else?" she provoked deliberately.

"It wouldn't have made any difference!" He cradled her in his arms and started toward the steps. Now what? Wasn't he going to make love to her, after all?

"Joel?" she questioned, her eyes flying up to meet his.

"I may be a brute in some respects, but I'm not such a selfish one that I'd inflict this kind of risk on a woman," he declared thickly as he carried her out of the water.

She shivered against him, but Shelley didn't know for certain if it was because of the desert breeze caressing her damp skin or if it was because of incipient disappointment. "That's—that's very thoughtful of you," she began unevenly, not at all sure she was really gratified by his restraint. Her body was throbbing with longing, and she wanted him in a way she'd never wanted any other man. The emotions coursing through her were enough to make even an intelligent woman such as herself take stupid risks.

He stared down at her suddenly rigid body in his arms, and then he appeared to realize what she was thinking. "There seems to be a slight misunderstanding here," he teased, mouth curving up gently at the corners. "Just because some people do not exercise forethought and planning in all aspects of their lives doesn't mean all of us are guilty of such oversights."

"Oh," she got out, strangely embarrassed, and buried her warm face in his shoulder.

"Don't worry, sweetheart. I'll take care of everything," he continued, hugging her close. "Will you mind making love to me in a conventional bed instead of the pool?"

"No," Shelley said in a small, muffled voice. Her body trembled with renewed anticipation.

He kissed the top of her head and carried her through another glass door that opened onto the bedroom. In the shadows Shelley caught a glimpse of a wide bed, a bookcase and assorted other furnishings, all done in the woods and natural fabrics of the other part of the house. The floor he paced across was polished wood, and there was a thick-piled area rug beside the bed.

"We're—we're dripping all over the rug, Joel," she pointed out nervously.

"It'll survive." He set her on her feet. "I'll be right back." After disappearing into the adjoining bathroom, he re-emerged a moment later with two huge bath sheets patterned in brown and white stripes. Wrapping one around his hips, he engulfed her in the other, massaging her dry with a caressing touch that set her skin tingling.

They were both trembling by the time the drying was finished, and Shelley's senses responded almost violently to the obvious signs of his need and passion. She touched him lightly, feeling the strength of him, glorying in the play of muscles beneath tanned flesh. Joel turned back the bed, picked her up and tenderly set her down in the middle. Then he was beside her, whispering his desire for her into the sensitive hollow of her ear.

Strong hands moved over her from ankle to throat, learning and possessing every place in between.

"There is a part of you that I didn't succeed in drying," he groaned as his fingers trailed urgently to the juncture of her legs. "Soft and moist and welcoming."

"Joel, I need you," she murmured, and knew she had never meant those lover's words when she had been married the way she meant them now with this near-stranger. In the morning, she told herself, she would sort it all out. Right now she could only surrender to the pull of this unbearable attraction.

"You couldn't need me half as much as I need and want you," he declared thickly. With a reluctant movement he lifted himself up on one elbow and fumbled with the drawer of the night stand. He trapped her languidly shifting legs with one strong thigh while he went through the masculine ritual designed to protect her, and then he was moving to overwhelm her body and fit her to him.

"Oh, Joel!"

She arched into his hardness, feeling the promising thrust of him as he came in contact with her welcoming flesh. But he held off a moment longer, raining kisses across her breasts and teasing her with tantalizing little thrusts that never quite entered until she thought she would go out of her mind.

"Joel, please! Joel, I need you!"

She used her teeth with punishing sharpness on his shoulder, raking her nails lightly down his back until she could sink them into the muscular curve of his buttock.

He groaned and responded to the sensuous punishment with a slow surge against her body. Shelley shivered and accepted his invasion eagerly, making Joel draw in his breath with a harsh, ragged sound.

"Shelley! My God, Shelley . . ."

He gathered her tightly to him, initiating a driving rhythm that began to tighten an already taut spring in Shelley's body. The pattern of his lovemaking became the pattern of the world they were creating around them. Nothing else mattered. Shelley clung to him, circling his lean waist with her legs and crying out her passion in gasping little breaths.

As the culmination approached, Joel caught her hips and anchored them still for a moment while he slowly withdrew from her body.

Shelley thought she would lose her sanity altogether. The tension within her demanded release. She would not let him tease and taunt her now!

"Joel," she begged, digging her nails savagely into his shoulders. "Joel, *love* me!"

"Yes!" he exclaimed, and surged masterfully back into her, dazzling her senses with his power. She felt the explosions of ecstasy ricocheting through her, convulsing her muscles in waves of thrilling completion, and before they had ceased, she heard his own hoarse shout of satisfaction and triumph as he locked himself to her in fulfilled passion.

After that there was a long, blissful, languorous silence that they floated through together just as they had floated in the crystal waters of the pool much earlier. Shelley allowed herself to surface slowly, finding the enticement of curling red chest hair delightfully near her fingertips when she opened her eyes. Joel was lying beside her, cuddling her close. She wrinkled her nose against the tickle of the crisp hair and dropped a butterfly kiss on him.

He stirred, chuckling indulgently. "That tickles."

"Grin and bear it," she ordered, giggling.

He laughed and slapped her thigh admonishingly. "Enough, woman!" he ordered softly, pulling her deeper into the strong circle of his arms.

She found she was in a contented, unbelievably happy state of mind. No thoughts of the past or the future were allowed to intrude. They existed, but they would be dealt with later. Much later. Shelley yawned delicately against his chest.

"Not falling asleep on me already, are you?" he complained.

"I was thinking about it, yes."

"Not yet, honey. I have a better idea." He sat up and lifted her back into his arms.

"Another swim?" she inquired, looking up at him through her drowsy lashes.

"Another everything."

"Oh. Amazing."

"Not so amazing when you think about the practical side of the matter," he informed her severely as he strode out onto the patio. "I figure the chlorine will disinfect some of the wounds you left upon my fragile body."

"Wounds!" She struggled in his arms, suddenly contrite as she tried to peer around at the broad shoulders to which she had been clinging so desperately. "Joel, did I really hurt you?"

"Let's just say it's lucky for me you're not into whips and leather."

She smiled placidly. "I'll bet you're secretly thrilled by the aggressive type."

"What thrills me," he stated quite clearly as he walked down the steps and into the inviting waters of the pool, "is having you explode like a burst of fireworks in my hands. You're high-energy stuff, Shelley Banning."

"As good as a video game?" she challenged lightly, feeding on his sensual praise as avidly as a hummingbird at a flower. Whatever lay ahead in their relationship, she would always have tonight, and she found herself clinging as fiercely to the moment as she had clung to his hard, driving body.

He shook his head, and some of the steel came back into his eyes as he looked down at her in his arms. "There's at least one major difference, sweetheart," he drawled with lazy emphasis. "Men stand in line to play video games. I'll be the only male standing in your line. You're mine now, and I won't be sharing you with any other man."

5

The phone call from Nina Winslow caught Shelley in the middle of a review of the Ackerly Manufacturing budget. She dropped everything after her friend's first words.

"Can you meet me for lunch, Shelley? I've got some news for you."

"Ralph proposed?" Shelley chuckled.

"Of course Ralph didn't propose. Ralph will never propose. You know that. I have also decided I don't want him to, anyway. No, this is business. It concerns your new client."

"Ackerly?" Shelley frowned thoughtfully, tapping the pencil in her fingers restlessly on her desk top.

"Yes. Frankly, I'd rather not say anything else over the phone. Can you get away around one o'clock?"

"You bet. That little sandwich place that has the salad bar?"

"Fine. I'll see you at one," Nina said briskly, and hung up the phone.

For a long moment Shelley sat at her desk staring into the middle distance and mulling over the possible news Nina had for her. Nina Winslow was a successful Phoenix real estate broker. Nearing forty, she was an energetic, hard-working woman with a flair for making money in her chosen field. More of a flair than several of her competitors. Because of her role in the business community she often had inside knowledge of important real estate deals before they were made public. It had been Nina who had told her about Joel's coup with the large California conglomerate.

A few minutes before one, Shelley left her office and stepped out into the warm Arizona afternoon. The city sprawled away from her toward the distant mountains, a lively combination of its Indian, western, and East Coast business heritages.

Nina arrived at the friendly little sandwich and salad restaurant a few minutes after Shelley. She came through the door with her usual dynamic stride, her handsome features framed by a cloud of silvering black hair. Nina's suit was expensive, fashionable and very tailored, just like the rest of her. She spotted Shelley at once and started toward the small table in the corner where her friend sat waiting with two glasses of white wine.

Often when she looked at Nina, Shelley saw her own future. Nina, she knew, had been through two unsuccessful marriages before declaring that she was giving up on the institution. She devoted herself to her career and maintained a series of short-lived affairs. Was that what she would be doing by the time she was forty? Shelley wondered with a pang of sadness. In the past, she had not allowed the string of dating relationships to evolve into full-blown affairs, but after last night she could no longer make that claim.

Was Joel a harbinger of the life-style she would be living in her thirties? She shivered, remembering his passion during the night and his farewell that morning as he'd driven her, first back to her own home so that she could change clothes and then on to the office.

"I'll call you this afternoon," he'd told her as he'd parked the white Maserati at the curb in front of her office building and leaned across the seat to pull her briefly but fiercely into his arms. "You and I are going to have to do some talking, woman."

She'd nodded and slid breathlessly out of the car, turning to lift a casual hand in farewell before escaping into the safety of the high-rise building. They had been late getting up that morning, and there had been little chance for conversation during the rush to get her home and then to the office. But the satisfaction and anticipation in Joel's eyes from the moment he'd awakened her would have made a serious, logical discussion difficult, anyway. Shelley wondered how Nina handled her affairs. Did knowing they were destined to end lessen the excitement of the beginning? How did a woman learn to deal with that foreknowledge?

But Nina was all business as she approached the table. Swinging her oversized handbag down with relief, she reached for the glass of wine Shelley had ordered and sipped before she was even fully seated.

"God! I needed that. What a day this has been! Sorry I'm late, Shelley."

"No problem. Shall we get our salads and then talk?"

Nina nodded enthusiastically, and together they went through the extensive salad-bar line with the skill and precision of professional dieters. After the way Joel had been stuffing her with food for the past two evenings, Shelley knew she was overdue for the restrictions of a salad luncheon.

"A successful day, Nina?" she asked in a friendly fashion as they carried the plates of greens back to the table.

"I was running around all morning like a deranged chicken trying to close that deal on the tennis ranch, but I think it's in the bag now," Nina explained, sinking into her chair again with a small sigh.

"Congratulations." Shelley carefully worked the single tablespoon of salad dressing she had allowed herself into the farthest reaches of the lettuce.

"Thanks, but I didn't call you in order to boast." Nina took another swallow of her wine. "Remember that California group of investors I told you about when you asked me if I'd ever heard of Joel Cassidy?"

"I remember. You had just heard about the real estate deal they had concluded with him."

"Well, I hear they're on the move again. And this time they're looking at some land Ackerly Manufacturing owns," Nina declared.

"You're kidding!" Shelley paused with a forkful of salad halfway to her mouth and slowly lowered it. "One of Ackerly's manufacturing sites?"

"That's the word I got. That parcel outside of Scottsdale."

Shelley froze, staring at her friend. "That *particular* site? They're interested in acquiring it?"

"I'm not positive of the details," Nina confessed briskly. "There's nothing firm about it, but another broker who has some dealings with the group said they were beginning to ask questions about the Ackerly site."

"No one's approached Ackerly as far as I know," Shelley noted with a frown.

"It will probably be done through the same broker who

worked on the Cassidy deal. I thought you might appreciate the advance warning on behalf of your client. I know you said the firm was in trouble. If that California group is serious, they'll offer top dollar. They're not quibbling about money. Maybe the sale of the site would be a help to Ackerly in its present financial difficulties?"

"What do you mean by offering top dollar?" Shelley whispered, staring at the golden wine in her glass as she tried to think through the situation.

"Half a million is my guess," Nina offered casually.

"Half a million dollars," Shelley repeated unbelievingly. "Nina, this is incredible. A sale of that magnitude could do a great deal to help Ackerly consolidate its financial position. There's just one very small, very interesting catch."

"Which is?" Nina cocked an interested eyebrow as she attacked her salad with the gusto she attacked everything else, including men and business.

"That *particular* parcel of land, together with the outdated manufacturing facilities on it," Shelley explained in a hard little voice, "just happens to be the Ackerly Manufacturing asset Phil Ackerly used to secure a loan he got from Joel Cassidy last year."

Nina chewed vigorously for a moment, swallowed and then said very dryly, "Interesting."

"Isn't it just?"

"Then Ackerly would not be free to sell that parcel for half a million to the California group?"

"Nope. Not at the moment," Shelley murmured thoughtfully as she tried to put together the pieces of the puzzle in her mind. "Ackerly can't do anything with that land until it pays off the money it owes Joel Cassidy."

"Of course," Nina observed very deliberately as she followed the line of reasoning to its logical conclusion, "Ackerly could surrender the parcel to Cassidy and get out from under the loan entirely."

"Whereupon Cassidy could then turn around and sell a piece of land he acquired for a hundred thousand dollars to the California investors for five hundred thousand dollars. A nice return on his money," Shelley concluded bleakly.

"Is Cassidy pushing for repayment of the loan? Trying to force Ackerly to hand over the land?"

Shelley shook her head wonderingly. "For some reason, he's agreed to give us more time to repay the loan. That doesn't make sense, does it?" She looked at her friend uncertainly.

"Who knows?" Nina shrugged. "Maybe he's confident Ackerly will never be able to pay off the loan and he'll eventually get the land, regardless."

"Games," Shelley said under her breath.

"What?"

"Games. The man's an expert at games of all kinds. Makes his living off them."

"I see what you mean. You think he might be playing a very sophisticated sort of game with you and Ackerly Manufacturing?" Nina hazarded perceptively.

"I don't know, Nina. I just don't know. I thought . . ." Her words trailed off as the memory of the night returned. Dear God, surely he wouldn't, surely he *couldn't* be playing a game with her? Don't be an idiot, she told herself grimly in the next instant. What did she know about Joel Cassidy to make her think he might *not* be predisposed to play such games? Not much. Only that he made love with a passion that seemed entirely honest. But perhaps he was entirely capable of combining passion and business. He'd said as much, hadn't he? He'd said he could make love to a business partner or do business with a lover.

But this would hardly qualify as doing business! This—this manipulation of herself and Ackerly Manufacturing amounted to something much more lethal than ordinary business dealings!

On the other hand, if his goal was to get hold of that chunk of Ackerly land, why would he agree to extend the loan? Shelley's head was beginning to spin with the various possibilities.

"Shelley, old pal, correct me if I'm wrong, but I get the feeling you've just seen a ghost." Nina frowned at her worriedly.

"Or an alien invader from space," Shelley clarified absently as she tried to focus on the problem. "The question is, Do I have the skill to defend the planet successfully?"

"Is this obscure accounting jargon?" Nina chuckled.

"That's game-playing jargon, Nina. I seem to find myself in the middle of a very complicated puzzle with no handy set of rules."

"I'm the bearer of bad tidings, aren't I?" Nina groaned in commiseration.

"They say it's better to be forewarned so that one can then be forearmed." Shelley tried to keep her tone firm and brisk. "Thanks for telling me what you found out about that conglomerate, Nina. You've been a great help. If I can ever do you a favor, you know you have only to ask," she added with genuine appreciation.

Nina smiled. "I know that, Shelley."

If only, Shelley thought ruefully, she had learned this piece of information before she had allowed herself to be seduced by Joel Cassidy. The uneasy regret made her fingers tremble slightly as she picked up her fork and went back to work on the salad in front of her.

What was going through Joel's head today? Self-congratulation? Was he whistling contentedly to himself as he worked on a pinball machine, thinking how he had Ackerly's accountant neatly in the palm of his hand?

Shelley winced. But why should he agree to extend the loan? Or had he done so because he was afraid that, if pushed, Ackerly might somehow find the hundred thousand dollars and not be forced to turn over the land? Had he decided it would be better to give Ackerly Manufacturing a little more rope to make certain it would indeed hang itself before demanding the asset that had been used to secure the loan?

What a mess! And now she'd been stupid enough to involve herself emotionally in the elaborate game being played with Ackerly Manufacturing. Shelley castigated herself mentally for the grievous error all the way back to her office.

"There you are, Shelley." Carol Robinson greeted her brightly as she walked into the reception area of Mason Wells & Associates. "You've had a couple of phone calls from Joel Cassidy." She handed Shelley the messages. "He wants you to call him back at that number when you get the chance."

Shelley stared down at Carol's scrawled messages and nodded, lifting her eyes obliquely to the younger woman, who smiled back at her.

"He sounded much nicer on the phone today than he did yesterday when he barged in here and demanded to see you immediately." Her attractive brown eyes lit up with amusement as she tossed her dark curls. "He seemed more polite today."

"Perhaps you succeeded in terrorizing him yesterday," Shelley offered in a vague attempt at humor.

"Who knows? More likely his lady friend was extra nice to him last night," the receptionist shot back unconcernedly as she returned to her typewriter.

Renewed interest in the letter she was typing kept her from seeing the wave of red that washed into Shelley's face. The day was deteriorating rapidly, she thought grimly as she hurried toward the privacy of her own office. When she passed another of the Mason Wells accountants in the hall, she didn't even bother with more than a brisk nod. The last thing she wanted was a casual chat. She felt like a small, cornered animal that wants only to hide from approaching predators.

When she reached her office, she slammed the door quickly and tossed the messages from Joel into the trash can. She needed desperately to think before she had any more dealings with Joel Cassidy.

The phone calls began to come with regular frequency after two o'clock. Carol put the first one through to Shelley with automatic assurance.

"It's Joel Cassidy again, Shelley. I've got him on line three."

"Tell him I'll call back when I'm free," Shelley said grimly into the intercom.

"I'm sorry, Shelley. I thought you were available!" Carol sounded so instantly contrite, Shelley wanted to relent. But discretion played a larger role in her life at the moment. She had been far too *indiscreet* last night!

"That's okay, Carol. I'm just a little tied up at the moment."

"Okay, I'll tell him."

The calls started coming every twenty minutes after that, and with each succeeding call Carol's mood went from cheerful to confused to plain curious. By the time she had completed the unpleasant task of trying to explain that Shelley Banning was unavoidably tied up in her office for the eighth time, Carol was ready to demand an explanation.

"Start telling him I'm out of the office if it's getting too difficult to tell him I'm busy," Shelley advised when Carol finally confronted her.

"*Lie* to him?" she gasped. "I don't think he's going to like that, Shelley. He's beginning to sound downright surly."

"Probably because the beneficial effects of the attentions he received from last night's lady love are wearing off," Shelley suggested with a trace of bitterness she couldn't quite hide.

If Carol was beginning to have her own suspicions about who the lady with Joel might have been last night, she wisely refrained from voicing them.

"What am I to tell him if he shows up in front of my desk in another hour?" she demanded instead.

With sudden decision, Shelley stood up and began stuffing some papers into her briefcase. "You can tell him I've left for the day. It will be the truth!"

"Oh." Helplessly, Carol watched the one member of Mason Wells & Associates whom she hadn't yet labeled "temperamental" walk out of the office in high dudgeon.

By the time she reached her yellow Toyota in the office parking lot, Shelley knew for certain where she was headed for the rest of the afternoon. It was time Dean Ackerly learned about the potential gold mine he was sitting on and couldn't yet sell. It was time he learned they might both be pawns in the high-stakes game Joel Cassidy was playing.

The game he *might* be playing, Shelley couldn't resist correcting herself as she drove through the sprawling suburbs of Phoenix toward the main headquarters of Ackerly Manufacturing. There was still a chance Joel was dealing a straight hand with her. After all, he had consented to extend that loan. So many "ifs," she thought ruefully. So many unknowns.

At Ackerly headquarters she announced herself to the receptionist, who sent her straight upstairs to the office of the new president. There again she was waved along until she found herself in Dean Ackerly's plushly carpeted, elegantly paneled suite. Shelley hid a small frown as he rose with alacrity to seat her. Attired in a light-colored linen-weave business suit and surrounded by such handsome furnishings, he appeared to command fully as much financial power as Joel Cassidy; it was difficult to remember that he was, in fact, in debt to the pinball mechanic to the tune of a hundred thousand dollars. Life, Shelley told herself reflectively, was not always fair.

"Shelley, I'm delighted to see you. I had no idea you were going to drop by this afternoon. If you're here for those inventory records, I can probably call downstairs and have them hurried along," Dean began a little anxiously.

"That's not why I'm here," she told him with a reassuring smile. "I won't need them until the first part of next week. This has to do with something else entirely."

Quickly, she told him what she had learned at lunch, keeping her voice smooth and businesslike. Not for the world did she want Dean to guess how involved she had managed to get with Cassidy in the course of forty-eight hours!

When she was through, he sat back in his padded leather chair with a murmured exclamation of incredulity. "I'll be damned. What a crazy situation. All that money almost in Ackerly's grasp and we can't quite reach out and take it."

"Not as long as it's being used as collateral on the Cassidy note," Shelley agreed with a short nod. "Remember, too, that these are just rumors," she added hastily. "There might not be any truth in them."

"What's your best guess?" he charged, leaning forward to rest his elbows on his desk and fix her with a narrowed gaze.

"My best guess is that the information is solid. The source is reliable."

"What about the possibility of paying off the Cassidy loan and stalling the bank for a while? If the conglomerate came through with an offer of half a million, we could then pay off the bank, too!"

"I don't think the bank will stall, Dean," Shelley said honestly. "And we don't yet have that offer in hand, either. If we did, there might be some negotiating we could do." Shelley broke off, trying to work out the possibilities in her mind.

"When do you think the offer will come?" Dean asked flatly, watching her intently.

"Who knows? Maybe never. At least not to us."

"What's that supposed to mean?"

Shelley drew a deep breath. "Dean, the big question in all this is, What does Joel Cassidy have in mind? I'm just not sure where he fits in."

"Are you trying to tell me he might be manipulating this whole situation?" Dean surged to his feet and walked restlessly toward the window.

"There is that chance," she told him baldly. "We know he was involved with the same conglomerate on a huge deal a few months ago. At that time, he may have discovered that they were also interested in the Ackerly land he was holding as collateral. He may have known about their potential interest in that land a year ago when he made the loan to your father! How do I know?" she grated fiercely. "He may have told them he has a claim on it and that he'll sell it to them when he takes possession!" Her mouth turned downward in self-disgust. How could she have been so stupid?

"If he wanted to take possession, why did he extend the loan?" Dean asked reasonably enough.

"I don't know, Dean. I just don't know. Unless he thought we might somehow manage to pay him off instead of turning over the land. Maybe he thinks that with my expert assistance you will actually find yourself in bankruptcy, after all. Or perhaps when he thinks we're desperate enough, he'll offer to buy the land from you for a paltry sum plus cancellation of the loan. Who can second-guess him?"

"We can't second-guess him, but we could try asking him exactly what he's got in mind," Dean murmured thoughtfully.

Shelley looked up in surprise, staring at Dean's back. "Could we trust his answer? That's the problem."

"Wheels within wheels," Dean groaned.

"Games," Shelley corrected ruefully. "Complicated games." She got to her feet purposefully. "Dean, I'm going to go home and try to sort this mess out. I want to have all the facts straight before we do anything as rash as confronting Cassidy and asking him what he's up to. I need a little time to map everything out on paper and draw up some contingency plans in case he's manipulating things for his own benefit. I'll check back with you tomorrow with some realistic scenarios we can work with, okay?"

He smiled wryly. "Okay. I'll rely on you to put everything in perspective, Shelley. In the meantime, I'll alert a few key members of my staff. Maybe all together we can come up with a way of resolving this to Ackerly's benefit!"

"We will!" she vowed with a resolution she wasn't sure she really felt. Leave 'em confident and thinking positive, she reminded herself as she returned his smile and headed for the door.

"Shelley?"

She paused, hand on the knob, and glanced back inquiringly. "Thanks," Dean said simply. "Your advance warning might make all the difference."

In spite of her brave words to her client, however, Shelley wasn't seeing the complicated situation in any clearer light by the time she had parked her car in the drive and let herself into the cool, inviting interior of her home. With a persistent frown of concentration, she crossed the champagne-colored carpet toward her bedroom where she changed from her business clothes into a pair of snug, faded jeans and a loose-fitting, exotically patterned shirt in saffron and purple.

Barefooted, she padded out into the kitchen and rummaged in the refrigerator for a grapefruit. A few minutes later, with the sectioned grapefruit perched on a small dish, she wandered back out into the living room.

Shelley glanced at the bulging briefcase waiting for her beside the desk in front of the window, but it was the puzzle table that drew her for some reason. She stood staring down at the unfinished scene of Venice and then reached idly for a piece to insert into the gondola.

What was Joel up to? What game was he playing with her? Could a man make love to a woman the way he had made love to her last night and still be intent on using her? Slowly, Shelley sank down into one of the ladderback chairs and picked up another piece of the jigsaw puzzle. She should be working on the contingency plans she had promised Dean Ackerly, but somehow it was easier to think while fiddling with the game in front of her.

Resolving the problem with Ackerly Manufacturing was similar to doing an especially difficult puzzle: there were too many unknowns to sort out and piece together. But one had to start somewhere. Take the first identifiable factor and search patiently for the next one.

Fact number one: Joel was a financially successful man, and he was a self-made man. That meant he was astute, quick to take advantage of a situation and use it to his own ends. People didn't start out with nothing and wind up controlling the kind of money Joel Cassidy controlled unless they always kept an eye out for the main chance. Such a man was capable of using people.

Fact number two: he made love with passion and integrity. He could have finished what he had started last night in the pool without stopping to concern himself over her welfare. But he had shouldered the responsibility of protecting her without any reluctance, as if it were his duty as her lover.

Fact number three: he knew and had worked with the California land investors. There was every reason to think he was still doing so. He had made more than one brilliant move in real estate during the past few years, according to Nina Winslow. The notion that he might be maneuvering to sell the Ackerly parcel to the conglomerate had to be accepted. He probably knew that the real value of the property was five times what he would have to pay for it if Ackerly went into bankruptcy. It would be his for the price of the hundred-thousand-dollar loan he had made to Phil Ackerly.

Fact number four: he had agreed to extend that loan while Shelley tried to rescue the faltering firm.

Shelley picked up another jigsaw piece and searched the board for the correct location. She was about to slide it into place when the doorbell rang. Reluctantly, she went to answer it even though she had a strong suspicion as to whom she would find waiting on the other side of the threshold. With a sense of gathering doom, she opened the door.

Joel stood there cradling a sack of groceries in each arm. He was wearing his work clothes, and the blue eyes traveled over her defiant expression with sardonic intent.

"Some men," he announced in a cool drawl, "might be offended at getting the cold shoulder from the woman they had spent the night with. Some men, a lesser sort of man, you understand, might feel hurt or annoyed or enraged. There are men in this world who, if they had spent the entire afternoon trying to call their lover, only to be told she couldn't talk to them, might resort to violence."

Shelley blinked warily, taking a step back. He took advantage of the opportunity to walk into the Spanish-tiled hall. "Joel," she tried to say firmly.

"A certain breed of male might consider beating a woman for treating him as if he were unimportant after she'd had her wicked way with him." He stalked past her toward the kitchen where he set the grocery bags down onto the counter with a touch of restrained violence. He swiveled to face her, feet braced slightly apart, his hands on his hips. The steel fairly glittered in the depths of his gaze as he swept her figure.

"Joel, I was very busy this afternoon." Shelley was horrified to hear herself begin the weak excuse. She had no need to invent any excuses, damn it!

"There are men in this world who don't accept excuses from their women because there *are* no reasonable excuses for what amounts to downright rude and cruel behavior!"

"Damn it, Joel, there are women in this world who don't see any need to make excuses for not being at a man's beck and call just because he did her the honor of spending the night with her!" Shelley flared, her own hands curving into small fists that she planted on her hips as she faced him. She was not going to let him put her on the defensive like this! He was the one whose actions were under suspicion!

"A lesser man than myself might really lose his temper over a statement like that. He might be tempted to put his woman over his knee and whale the living daylights out of her. It might not effect a large measure of behavior modification, but it sure as hell would relieve a certain amount of his frustration!"

"Joel!"

"But you, Shelley Banning, are an exceedingly lucky female," he declared, dropping his hands from his hips and turning back to the grocery sacks, "because you are involved with not just any man."

"How fortunate!" she exclaimed, enraged.

"Isn't it?" he murmured unperturbed. He reached into one sack and removed a chunk of Parmesan cheese and a package of pasta. "Yes, indeed, you have had the good fortune to get involved with a man who understands you. He knows you're scared to death about what happened last night. He comprehends your fear of getting emotionally entangled with a business associate, and he understands your fears of finding yourself involved so thoroughly and so quickly with a man. He is also perceptive enough to realize exactly what's wrong with you this evening!"

"And what might that be, Joel Cassidy?" she demanded.

"Why that you haven't had a proper meal all day, naturally. Everyone knows women get testy when they haven't had a good meal." He hauled a few more items out of the grocery sacks, including a bottle of Chianti Classico, a bunch of romaine lettuce and some cream.

"Joel, just what do you think you're doing?"

"I'm going to feed you," he said simply, opening a cupboard door and hunting around inside until he found a large kettle. "And you, if you have the sense you were born with, will start grating the Parmesan cheese. If you don't, I might get upset and revert to the behavior one might expect from a less understanding man. In other words, I might throttle you!"

She heard the underlying tension in his words and bit her lip against the retort she was about to make. "Joel, I've already had dinner," she heard herself say instead.

"If you're talking about that little grapefruit I saw on

the puzzle table, that barely qualifies as an appetizer. Get to work on the Parmesan, woman. Hunger can take its toll on a man's temper, too, you know!"

Half an hour later, he put the plate of fettucine Alfredo down in front of Shelley and took the chair across from her at the round pedestal table in the dining area. "Now," he growled gently as he poured the Chianti, "do you want to talk about today?"

"Joel, I had a rough day," Shelley said very steadily, eyeing the pasta with a hunger she knew was dangerous.

"So did I. At one point, I was tempted to storm into the offices of Mason Wells & Associates and carry off one of their accountants across my saddle bow. Every time I called and was told you'd get back to me and you didn't, I kept reminding myself that you were probably scared as hell." He snagged her wary gaze across the table and said deliberately, "Don't be afraid of me, Shelley. I keep telling you, I *understand* you. And I'm not afraid of you. Your ambition and your skills and your desire for success don't frighten me in the least."

Shelley stared at him, a surge of longing welling up into her throat. She wanted to confront him with the news she'd had that day, wanted to ask him what sort of game he was playing with Ackerly Manufacturing and with her. But it was too soon. There was a client involved, and she owed it to the struggling manufacturing firm to protect its best interests. Confronting Joel point-blank and asking for an explanation would give him the advantage of knowing they were aware of the true value of the parcel of land. If he really were scheming, it might cause him to act quickly to ensure his possession of the property. At the moment, she had some time in which to maneuver on behalf of Ackerly. Shelley knew she couldn't jeopardize her slender advantage for personal reasons. She had no right to do that.

So it was easier and less risky to fall back on what he

thought was the real reason she had been refusing his calls all day.

"Joel, just because we—we spent the night together, that doesn't give you the right to assume too much about our relationship."

"It sure as hell does," he shot back smoothly. "I thought I made it very clear last night that I consider you mine. I staked a claim on you last night, sweetheart, and I'm fully capable of retaining possession. I am a very understanding man," he added with a note of husky warning, "but you pushed that understanding to the limits today. *Don't ever again do to me what you did to me this afternoon!*"

Shelley felt suddenly chilled.

"The next time you're upset, scared or suspicious of me, you will do me the courtesy of facing me and talking out the situation. Is that very clear?" he went on deliberately.

"Joel!" That was exactly what she wanted to do, Shelley thought bitterly, but she didn't dare. Not yet; too much was at stake. She couldn't run the risk of having him lie to her. Damn! but it had been a mistake to mix business and passion. What a fool she had been!

"Because if it's not clear, I will be happy to tattoo it in words of one syllable someplace very obvious on your soft body!" he concluded grimly.

"It's clear," Shelley muttered, and stabbed vengefully at the fettucine.

What wasn't at all clear was how she was going to cope with this lethal combination of desire and business. A mistake in either sphere would ruin her.

6

Shelley was at her desk in her office the next morning long before any of the rest of the staff arrived. She was on her second cup of coffee by the time she heard other people in the reception area, and she kept her door firmly closed so that none of her co-workers would be tempted to stop in for a morning chat.

Shelley had no time for morning chats; she was trying to detail the various contingency plans she had promised Dean Ackerly. The plans that should have been roughed out at her desk at home last night.

It wasn't Joel's fault the plans hadn't gotten done, at least not directly, she was forced to admit as she paused to sip coffee and study her progress. He hadn't attempted the seduction routine she had been expecting. He hadn't tried to stake his "claim" again. Much to her astonishment, Joel Cassidy had made himself comfortably at home for a couple of hours after dinner, working with her on the puzzle, listening to some Bach on the stereo and talking easily about everything from the amusement business to the weather.

Under the unthreatening flow of words and actions Shelley had finally relaxed enough to conduct something close to normal conversation. She had even relaxed sufficiently to start thinking about how to handle what she expected would be the inevitable conclusion of the evening. Her mind had begun to toy with rationalizations for succumbing once more to the passion Joel could generate between them.

But the rationalizations had proved totally unnecessary. Somewhere around ten o'clock, he had arisen from the puzzle table, stretched luxuriously and kissed her good-by. She had watched him climb into the white Maserati and drive off into the desert night with a strangely wistful sensation when she should have been feeling relieved or suspicious.

The wistfulness had made it impossible to work, and Shelley had told herself she would compensate by arising early the next morning and going into the office a couple of hours ahead of time. Then she had gone to bed and thought about Joel Cassidy far into the night.

Thus far this morning, her plan had worked, however. She had accomplished a great deal working with the possibility that the parcel of Ackerly land had far greater value than anyone had ever before assumed. She had drawn scenarios of how Ackerly could use an offer on that land to deal with the bank. She had formulated an outline of what they could do with the half million dollars, and she had considered the benefits and disadvantages to Ackerly of losing that particular manufacturing site.

On the whole, getting rid of the site might be very

beneficial. It was a more drastic move than either she or Dean had considered, but if the price was right, the end result of consolidation and belt tightening could be very useful.

By nine o'clock, she had convinced herself that she had wrung every possible alternative out of the situation and gotten them down on paper for presentation to Ackerly Manufacturing. Every possible alternative, that was, if one worked under the assumption that Joel Cassidy was not personally manipulating matters. If he were innocent of any scheming and the extension of the loan was merely a generous gesture on his part and if he knew nothing of the California conglomerate's interest in that land— If, if, if.

Shelley shook her head and picked up her pencil again. Now she had to go through the process of creating scenarios based on the other assumption: that Joel was conniving to make sure he got the land rather than his hundred thousand dollars. When she began working with the alternatives available to Ackerly in that case, things looked far more grim. The smart thing to do was to pay off Joel and get him out of the picture before he took possession of the land through bankruptcy or default on the loan.

But Ackerly couldn't afford to pay him off, not if they were to keep the bank pacified at the same time.

Her progress slowed considerably as she dealt with the dangerous possibilities if Joel were guilty of playing games. What was she to believe? Shelley asked herself again and again. How could she trust a man who made his living the way Joel did? A man she had been to bed with once and about whom she knew little except that he was a hustler in business and probably in every other area of life as well. The pencil in her hands snapped.

The small act of destruction startled her, and she sat

staring bleakly down at the two pieces of broken pencil. What was that man doing to her? How could she allow him to upset her work like this?

The thought was broken off as completely as the pencil stub when the intercom on her desk buzzed.

"There's a lady calling on line three, Shelley. She won't give her name. Shall I put her through? It sounds urgent," Carol advised briskly.

"Go ahead." Shelley picked up the phone curiously. "This is Shelley Banning. May I help you?"

"Miss Banning, you don't know me, and there's no reason to introduce myself except to say I'm an associate of Joel Cassidy's." The voice on the other end of the line was faint, a little breathless sounding. "What I wish to discuss with you concerns business only. Please do not interrupt. I will make this offer only once, and it will be very much in your best interests to pay careful attention."

Annoyed at the highhanded announcement, Shelley automatically started to interrupt, only to be cut off by the caller's next words.

"What I have to say involves a client of yours. Ackerly Manufacturing."

"I'm listening," Shelley said quietly, suddenly and totally alert. It might have been her imagination, but she could have sworn the premonition of danger made the hair rise on the back of her neck. Now what?

"Ackerly is headed for bankruptcy. Nothing you can do will halt that slide, and you would be well advised to remove yourself from the picture before your reputation suffers from association. The company will fail, Miss Banning. Let it go down on its own." The stranger sounded as if she were *reading*.

"What are you trying to say?" Shelley asked warily.

"If you remove yourself from the scene, you will find it worth your while. You will be adequately compensated for the loss of your client. Do you understand, Miss Banning? You will be compensated, but only if you stay out of Ackerly affairs."

Shelley swallowed in fury and sheer disbelief. "Are you trying to bribe me?" she whispered in astonishment.

"Your compensation for ridding yourself of this client will be most generous, Miss Banning. It will amount to far more than your normal salary. Think about it." The phone was replaced in the receiver on the other end with a sharp click.

Shelley sat glaring at the silent phone in her hand. A bribe! She had just been offered a bribe to give up the task of trying to salvage Ackerly Manufacturing. Who in his or her right mind would bother bribing an accountant?

Someone who wanted to be certain the company failed? Someone who stood to gain from Ackerly's slide into bankruptcy? The main candidate for that role at the moment was Joel Cassidy. It would be an easy way to acquire that land.

Fingers trembling with a strange kind of fear coupled with a fierce hurt and anger, Shelley gently hung up her phone. Would he do this to her? Could he do this to her? Was he capable of hiring someone to call her up and offer her a bribe to let Ackerly Manufacturing go to financial hell? Oh, dear God! If only she knew more about him. If only there had been more time to learn the true depths of her dangerous business associate.

Restlessly, she began to pace the small office. Why hadn't he offered the bribe himself? Why use someone else to do the dirty work? The answer was obvious, of course. He wouldn't want to jeopardize his own business reputation by such an act. But what would make him think she was open to a bribe?

Shelley halted in front of her window, frowning. He

knew that what was important to her in the Ackerly deal was the reputation she could make for herself, not the money. She shook her head dejectedly. More jigsaw pieces and none of them were fitting together.

The office became oppressive, and she walked over to her phone and dialed Dean Ackerly's number. She needed an excuse to get out of the building, and he was the logical one to use.

"Dean? I've got some facts and figures together. Have you got time to go over them?"

"Shelley, you know that under the present circumstances, any request from you automatically becomes my number-one priority!" He chuckled ruefully. "Do you want me to come over to Mason Wells?"

"No, I'll drive over to your office. See you in a few minutes."

Leaving word of her destination with Carol, Shelley left the building with one major question running through her head. How much should she tell Dean? She had no intention of accepting the bribe, so was there really any need for him to be aware the offer had been made?

Not yet, she whispered silently as she slid behind the wheel of her car. Not yet. It was an excuse, she knew. She should be keeping her client totally informed of events. But somehow she couldn't bring herself to further implicate Joel. She wanted to be certain he was at the bottom of this crazy game before she made any further accusations to Dean. Her fingers tightened on the steering wheel as she wondered frantically how she was going to learn the truth before it was too late.

Dean was ready and waiting with his vice president and top-level managers. Summoning her full executive demeanor, Shelley launched into a presentation of various alternative plans, discussion of which took up the remainder of the day. There was no problem keeping everyone's attention during the high-level meeting. The company was fighting for its corporate life. Dean's staff was ready and willing to work.

The questions came fast and furiously, and she dealt with them honestly, including the painful ones about Joel.

"Where does Cassidy fit into this?"

"What can we expect from Cassidy if we do get an offer from the California people? Will he let us make the deal and then pay him off, or will he demand to be paid first?"

"The half million could be exactly what we need to bail ourselves out of this mess. The question is, Will Cassidy let us get our hands on it?"

Shelley shook her head after each question. "Please keep in mind that we have yet to hear from the California group. There may not be any offer at all forthcoming. If we don't get the offer, we can hardly make a deal with either Joel Cassidy or the bank."

By the end of the day Shelley was exhausted. She was also, she discovered to her unlimited disgust, hungry. Joel had gotten her poor stomach back in the habit of eating. As the meeting broke up, she met Dean's eyes across the room.

"What do you say we adjourn for a martini?" he inquired casually as the last of his managers filed out of the room, mumbling to themselves. "I think we owe it to ourselves."

Shelley was on the verge of accepting when she saw the beginning of a deeper question in Dean Ackerly's eyes. No, she thought wildly, the last thing I need is another business involvement! She'd learned her lesson with Joel, hadn't she? Better to squelch that question in Dean's gaze at once.

"Thanks, but I'm hot and exhausted, Dean." She

smiled briefly. "If you don't mind, I think I'll just go home and throw myself into the pool and then have a quiet meal and go to bed. Thanks, anyway." She was halfway out the door by the time she'd finished her little speech.

"Another time, perhaps," he murmured politely, watching her go.

"Yes," she agreed, knowing she was lying through her teeth. If there was one thing she was certain of, it was that she would maintain only a business relationship with Dean Ackerly.

There would have been no point in pursuing anything else, anyway, she told herself as she drove home. A relationship with Dean would follow the same course as her other relationships had followed over the years. There would be a short period of mutual interest that would slowly deteriorate as he realized she expected as much respect for her career as he expected for his. When he pushed for intimacy, she would begin withdrawing, knowing there would be no long-term commitment and not wanting a sexual relationship without that commitment. Eventually, things would disintegrate altogether. He would never really understand her.

Joel Cassidy had been the exception to that pattern, and Shelley still could not justify her reaction to him. How could she have broken the safe routine of her relationships for such a man? A man who could ruin all of her career plans? A man who called her a hustler? A man who seduced her? A man who might have paid another woman to bribe her?

By the time she allowed that painful thought to re-emerge in her mind, Shelley was walking through the front door of her home. She did exactly what she had told Dean she was going to do. She changed into a black and white striped one-piece swim suit that she had bought because she thought the severe colors and striping made her look a little thinner, gathered up an oversized towel and a swim cap and headed for the pool in the center of the condominium complex.

As she sank blissfully into the refreshing water, she tried very hard not to think about how Joel had carried her in and out of the pool at his home. A few of her neighbors were doing the same as she, relaxing after a hard day, and she chatted pleasantly with them before beginning a series of laps that she hoped would drain some of the tension from her body.

It was rather effective therapy. As she moved back and forth in the water, Shelley's head began to clear, and she started thinking again. She wasn't going to sort out the mystery around Joel Cassidy by rehashing the few facts available to her.

Very well, she told herself as she came to the end of the pool and turned neatly underwater for the next lap, she couldn't predict Joel's role accurately. At this point in time, that much was a given fact. Today, with Dean Ackerly's staff, she had worked out various alternatives available to the firm once the future clarified itself. So what should she be doing in the meantime?

The answer came like a flash of lightning into her head as she surged up out of the water and grasped the far end of the pool's edge. It hit her the moment she blinked the water out of her hazel eyes and looked up to see Joel Cassidy standing in front of her.

For a second, they stared silently at each other, Joel's gaze shuttered and coolly assessing; Shelley's darkening to a golden green. The answer, she realized, was to be as cool and mysterious as he was. She would play his game and give away nothing. There would be no clues from her as to Ackerly's contingency decisions; nor would she allow him to realize just how wary she was of him. She would tell him nothing about the bribe, give him nothing to go on. He would find himself picking up the pieces of the jigsaw puzzle in the dark, just as she was having to do. She would start making a few of her own rules in this ruthless, dangerous game.

"You have a nasty habit of disappearing on a man," Joel finally remarked, breaking the silence as he crouched down in front of her. He was wearing the usual faded denims and blue shirt, and his heavy red hair gleamed faintly in the last rays of the sun. "I spent a good portion of the afternoon dialing your office, only to be told you were 'out.'"

"I was," she said simply, stripping off the bathing cap but making no move to pull herself up out of the water. She felt safer staying in the pool for the moment. "I was with a client," she clarified self-righteously.

"So I discovered when I finally got mad enough to drive over and see for myself," he retorted laconically. "I think that lady who sits at the front desk has taken a strong personal dislike to me."

"It must be your winning personality and dazzling smile." Shelley kept her voice light and supremely casual, adding just the right touch of mockery. She would keep this man dangling, exactly as he was doing to her. Two could manipulate the control panel of this particular war game.

"That's what it took to get her to tell me where you had gone. A winning personality and a dazzling smile. She finally admitted you were over at Ackerly Manufacturing."

"Nice of you not to barge in while I was with a client," she muttered, looking up at him from under her lashes while she tried to anticipate the next move.

"I wouldn't think of it. Just remember, I expect equal treatment. After all, I'm going to be a much bigger client than Ackerly in the long run. Assisting Ackerly Manufacturing will help give you a reputation. Being my accountant will give you a certain amount of sheer clout."

"Are you trying to bribe me, Mr. Cassidy?" she heard herself say before she had paused to think. Horrified at her slip of the tongue, Shelley went on hastily. "Trying to tell me it's going to be to my advantage to spend a little more time with you?" She winced inwardly. That remark wasn't much better!

His mouth crooked upward at the corner. "Want to hear me enumerate the advantages?" He seemed to be relaxing a little, perhaps because he had succeeded in locating her once again. Was he really spending a large portion of his days trying to keep tabs on her?

Shelley folded her arms on the edge of the pool and smiled up at him with mocking politeness. "Name one."

"You'll eat better."

"That's an advantage?"

"You'll have an opportunity to learn to defend the planet earth from a variety of alien invaders."

"Another dubious benefit," she murmured, kicking her feet idly behind her in the water.

"Plus," he concluded, leaning forward slightly as the crooked smile became something resembling a leer, "I'm good in bed and in a pool!"

Shelley felt the tips of her ears go red as she glared at him, outraged. How many of her neighbors around the pool had heard that remark? "Let's just see how good you really are in the water!"

That he was already leaning forward, a little off balance as he crouched so close to the edge, helped greatly. Shelley grasped his arm and heaved herself backward with a force that clearly took him by surprise.

Joel's astonished expression and the oath that was cut off as he landed in the pool with a splash were satisfaction enough for Shelley. But if ever there was a time for

strategic retreat, this was it. Hastily, she tried to scramble
safely up onto dry land, aware of the grinning faces
ringing the pool.

"Oh, no you don't!" With surprising agility, given the
fact that he was weighted down with water-heavy clothing, Joel grabbed her ankle and hauled her back into the
water. "Is that any way to treat an important client?" he
growled with laughing menace, and then he transferred
his grip from her ankle to her shoulders and dunked her
briefly.

"My hair!" she gasped in dismay when she sputtered
to the surface.

"Your hair is not as important as my pride. I think I
want a bit more respect from my accountant!"

"Yes, sir!" she drawled, thinking that he suddenly
looked a great deal happier than he had a few moments
ago. It was as if the playful roughhousing had reassured
him in some way. She liked seeing him happy, Shelley
realized fleetingly, and then told herself it was to her
benefit to keep him off guard and relaxed like this. Yes,
this was the way to play the game. She must keep him
unwary and unknowing.

"Much better," he approved, swimming with her to
the shallow end of the pool. He kept a firm grip on her
wrist as he hauled her out beside him. "Keep the client
happy. That should be your motto in the future."

"I'll remember that next time I'm talking to Dean
Ackerly," she said obligingly, and then wondered why
she had deliberately baited him like that.

"Why, Shelley, honey, are you by any chance trying to
make me jealous?" he asked interestedly as they paused
briefly to scoop up her towel.

"Do clients get jealous of each other?" she countered,
rubbing herself with furious energy and using the activity
as an excuse not to meet his piercing blue eyes.

"This one would if he thought the business relationship between you and Ackerly was in danger of growing into something more!" he told her crisply as she handed him the towel. After a moment, he gave up the fruitless attempt to dry himself and his clothing and draped the towel around his neck. "How are things going with Ackerly?" he inquired in a suspiciously conversational tone as he took her hand and started back across the grass in the direction of her condominium.

Shelley tried to assess what lay behind the question. Simple curiosity? Or was he deliberately trying to pump her for information? She had to go on the latter assumption, she told herself. She had to assume the worst if she was going to give Ackerly any measure of protection.

"Things are going fine. Don't worry; your money will be safe," she said carelessly.

"Still think you can salvage the firm?"

"We'll see." Shelley pretended a total lack of interest in the discussion. "I hope you didn't arrive with more food tonight, Joel. I already had a nice, low-calorie dinner planned."

"How low calorie?"

"A piece of dry toast and an egg," she told him grandly, relieved that he seemed willing to drop the Ackerly conversation. Perhaps he was wary of making her suspicious? It was all so complicated!

"That sounds awful. Lucky for you I exercised my usual foresight and planning abilities again this evening," he added cheerfully. "I am beginning to wonder if you can cook anything besides grapefruit or an egg, though."

"Of course I can cook! All dieters can cook, usually very well. How do you think they get into so much trouble in the first place?"

"Prove it." He grinned as they stepped through the kitchen door, and he knelt to remove his wet, sloshing shoes.

"How?" She eyed him challengingly.

"See what you can do with what I've got in the bag." He nodded toward the new grocery sack on her tiled counter. "By the way, you neglected to lock your front door earlier," he said in a reproving tone of voice. "I'm going to take a shower and get out of these wet clothes."

"Wait!" she interrupted hurriedly. "What will you put on afterward? I don't have a robe that would begin to fit you!"

"You should have thought of that before you pulled me into the pool," he told her kindly, beginning to unbutton the soaking shirt. Then he relented. "Have you got a dryer?"

"Oh, yes," she mumbled, embarrassed at having forgotten the obvious. It was the thought of Joel Cassidy's running naked around her apartment, using her shower and generally making himself too much at home, that had blanked her mind for a painful second, she decided regretfully. "You can use the shower in my bathroom. I'll use the guest bath," she added quickly, hurrying off. Now why in the world had she ordered him into the intimacy of her own bathroom? Damn it! It was growing more and more difficult to think clearly around Joel!

When he reappeared in her kitchen twenty-five minutes later with a towel wrapped around his lean waist, it was to pause and sniff the savory aromas in satisfaction.

"My God! You can cook! When do we eat?" He leaned over the simmering pot on the stove, and Shelley retreated a step from the clean, tanned expanse of naked flesh. He looked so good to her, appealed in such a fundamental way to her senses, she realized uneasily. How did one play it cool and stay in charge of a situation like this? Never had a man's mere presence had such an effect on her.

"We eat," she managed gamely, "as soon as you get properly dressed. Your clothes should be about done."

Twenty minutes later, she presented the chicken curry and brown rice with a flourish. Lined up in a neat array around the platter of curry were little bowls of various condiments: chutney, diced hard-cooked eggs, chopped celery, raisins, coconut and chopped black olives. To one side, a spinach salad in a clear glass bowl waited. As Joel took his seat with anticipation, she poured the pale-gold Chardonnay.

"All this out of that grocery sack?" he asked in amazement and awe.

"Some of it came out of some jars and cans I found buried in a cupboard," she confessed lightly. "I'd forgotten about the coconut and chutney I had stashed away."

"I take back any innuendo I may have made about your inability to cook," he told her after the first bite.

"You knew I'd respond to a challenge, didn't you? Are you always so good at manipulating situations and people, Joel?" She tasted the rich California wine and watched him over the rim of the glass as he helped himself to samples of each of the condiments.

"I manage to get by in this world," he said with blatantly false modesty.

"Yes, you do, don't you?" Why this desire to goad and provoke, she wondered silently. What was it about this man that kept luring her into dangerous areas?

"The next question," he informed her casually, "is, Do I get everything I want in this world? To which I then reply, Yes, if I want it badly enough. At which point, you will accuse me of arrogance, right?"

"You've just destroyed the next ten minutes of dinner

conversation," she pointed out with a sigh. "What will we talk about now?"

"Oh, I'm willing to stay with the subject a little longer." He met her eyes meaningfully and smiled invitingly. "I'm willing to take it the next logical step and tell you that what I want most in the world right now is you. Don't look so shocked. You knew it was coming, didn't you? I haven't made any secret about it." He helped himself to the spinach salad as she stared at him.

"You mean you expect to have an affair with me?" she forced herself to ask.

"I didn't want you to get the wrong idea just because I walked out last night. It took me all day to decide that was a mistake. Which is why I'm back tonight."

The spicy curry and the tangy chutney were quite tasteless in her mouth now. Shelley tried to rally her forces. She hadn't expected him to be quite this bold. At least not over dinner!

"Why did you walk out last night?" she tried to say disinterestedly.

"Some crazy notion that you needed a little time, I think. But when I spent another day trying to track you down again—"

"I was working! Not deliberately avoiding you!"

"I realize that," he responded gently. "But it also made me realize I want to know I can find you with some degree of certainty." He picked up his wine glass and swirled the contents reflectively. "I want you to come and live with me, Shelley Banning. I want to know where you'll be every night. I can stop driving myself crazy during the day if I know you'll be home when I get there."

Shelley slowly set down her fork, no longer able to make even a pretense of eating. Her nerves were vibrating with a thrill that was a combination of fear and longing. She seemed fated to know well those two emotions around this man.

"Do you want me to come and live with you for the duration of the time I'm responsible for your hundred thousand dollars?" she mocked tightly. "Is this a business arrangement you're offering, Joel?"

The steel hardened in the depths of his eyes, but his voice was quiet and purposeful. "We'll talk about it after dinner. The offer is obviously affecting your appetite, and I wouldn't want that."

"Joel," she began forcefully, determined to refuse the proposition once and for all.

"Eat, woman. And stop worrying about the future. I've already told you I tend to get much of what I want in life, so why fight the inevitable?"

"Now you're trying to provoke me!" she accused.

"You know you love a challenge," he murmured, his expression softening indulgently.

And what or whom do you love, Joel Cassidy? she wanted to ask with sudden fierceness, only to be shocked by the silent question. This man loved wheeling and dealing. He was a hustler; he'd admitted it. She didn't have to ask him if he was capable of love. She should be able to guess the answer immediately! Besides, she wasn't searching for love, anyway, was she? Shelley reminded herself that she'd tried to find it and had already learned the hard way that it was an elusive emotion probably not intended for women who were cursed with ambition and a desire for success. The divorce rate among the ambitious and successful women she knew was inordinately high, and she had been a statistic herself. Men did not understand or accept such women readily into the intimate side of their lives. They were willing to have brief affairs with such women because a dynamic, self-contained female was an exciting challenge. But Shelley knew as well as anyone that when the relationship progressed beyond that stage, there were grave risks.

So why was she tempted to take those risks with Joel Cassidy?

7

What she must keep in mind, Shelley told herself several times during the remainder of the meal, was that Joel was not exactly proposing marriage. Far from it. But she had the feeling that asking her to move in with him was more of a commitment on his part than it would have been coming from another man.

Or was she seeking excuses to succumb to the pull of the undeniable attraction between them?

Why was it that everything involving this man was so damn complicated, she thought ruefully as they cleared the table and wandered out into the living room.

"If we work hard, we can finish this puzzle tonight," Joel noted, standing beside the glass table and eyeing the unfinished portion critically. He munched a tart kumquat he had swiped from a bowl of fruit Shelley kept on the kitchen counter. The brilliantly colored, lemony-orange fruit disappeared into his mouth as he seated himself and reached for a piece of the jigsaw. "Sit down, honey, and let me tell you about my hard day."

Shelley stared down at the puzzle and thought that at the rate she was going, she might not find the solution to the real puzzle in her life until it was far too late. But she took the other chair, grateful for the distraction of the game in front of her.

For a time, they worked together in silence. Joel still had the unnerving habit of always seeking the particular bit of puzzle that fit whatever piece she had just found, but Shelley was getting used to the small, implied intimacy. Was she even beginning to welcome it? It was an extremely subtle form of pursuit, she told herself, and she must be careful.

"So tell me about your hard day," she suggested softly, her eyes on the game.

"Well, I got to the shop this morning to discover that one of the video games had gotten in the middle of a bar fight last night. A couple of thousand bucks' worth of machine shot to hell."

"Perhaps it was the calculated revenge of certain anonymous invaders from outer space."

"More likely a tavern full of anonymous truck drivers," he retorted dryly. "Anyhow, we sent another machine out to the location and retrieved the broken one. It's going to need a new card, new glass, new—"

"A new card?" She glanced up, confused.

"A new printed-circuit board," he explained. "Gone are the good old days when a man could fix a pinball machine with a screwdriver and a wrench. The insides of those new machines are like computers. Ah, well. The price of progress, I suppose. Where was I? Oh, yes. Shortly after that, I learned that one of my oldest locations, a bowling alley, has recently been sold and the new owner is talking about switching route operators."

"You mean you're going to lose the location?"

"The new owner, apparently, has worked before with Nick Sanders, a route operator across town, and wants him to supply the games at the bowling alley." Joel paused to select a rounded bit of puzzle and slip it into the curving piece Shelley had just placed.

"Does this mean a war over the video-game routes? Blood in the streets?" Shelley chuckled.

"It means that if I can't convince the new owner of the bowling alley that I'm an all-around nice guy and great to do business with, I will then have to call up Nick and invite him out for a beer. We will then proceed to amiably discuss our unspoken agreement to honor each other's territory. After which, he will explain to the new bowling alley owner that he'd like to service him but he just can't extend his route to the far side of town."

"And if good old Nick doesn't seem to recall this unspoken agreement," Shelley prodded interestedly, "then does it become war in the streets of Phoenix?"

"You have a rather nasty image of my chosen profession, don't you?" he complained. "Don't worry, I don't plan to go to war over a bowling alley! Nick and I will work something out. Along about then I started calling my accountant and began getting what I thought might be the same brush-off I got yesterday. My mood began to deteriorate rapidly."

"A rough life," she taunted gently.

"Isn't it though? Lucky for all of us you were home this evening when I finally decided to drop by and tell you I believed your receptionist this time and that I wasn't going to hold your unavailability this afternoon against you."

"I'm so relieved."

"You should be. If I hadn't decided to believe today's story, it really might have become a case of war in the streets of Phoenix. A man can only take so many frustrations in one day!" He found the chunk of sky that mated with hers and put it into place decisively before he glanced up with a pinning glance. "Enough about my bad day. Tell me about yours. How are things going with Ackerly?"

"No one said it would be easy, and it isn't," she responded lightly, refusing to look up and meet his eyes. She mustn't give him any solid information, but if she flatly refused to discuss the matter, he'd know she was on to something. He'd know; that is, she mentally corrected herself, if he had a reason to worry in the first place! She hunted for another piece of sky. The puzzle was almost finished now, with only a few bits of jigsaw left to insert.

"Have you had to modify any of the original battle plan?" he asked conversationally, putting down the piece he was holding in his fingers and getting to his feet to stroll toward the kitchen.

"Not really," she said, watching him with a slanting glance. Why did he have to be the one to capture her senses? Why was it Joel Cassidy who could hold her eyes just by crossing a room? She'd never in her life cared much one way or the other about red hair, but on this man it made her want to put out her hand and thread her fingers through the dull-red fire. "The plans I made are basic to the kind of corporate catastrophe in which Ackerly finds itself." There, that sounded loosely professional, didn't it?

Joel came back to the table carrying her good French cognac and two glasses. "Speaking of basic plans," he said quietly as he poured, "maybe now is the time for us to start talking about my—"

"Your proposition?" she supplied with quiet sarcasm.

He sat down abruptly and placed one glass in front of her. Under the male command in his eyes, she picked it up and took a cautious sip. He did the same, and then he set his snifter down very firmly.

"I want you, and you want me, Shelley. Come and live with me."

As if it were somehow an act of will she was exercising against the passionate demand in him, Shelley picked up the next to the last piece of puzzle and concentrated fiercely on putting it in place. But her gilded papaya-colored fingertips trembled a little as she worked.

Joel pounced without warning, leaning forward and catching hold of her hand just as she was about to reach for the last piece of the puzzle. He said nothing, willing her gaze up to meet his. Unable to do anything else, Shelley looked up and became enmeshed, as she had known she would be, in the steel-blue trap waiting for her.

"It's going to be okay, honey," he told her deeply.

Desperately, she struggled against the bonds of the snare in which she found herself. The small truce that had been in effect since dinner was clearly over. Joel was going after what he wanted. "It's too soon, Joel. There is so much we don't know about each other. So much to make certain of before taking that kind of step."

"Stop being afraid of me!" he rasped with impatience. "Shelley, we're so much alike in so many ways that being afraid of me can only mean you're afraid of yourself. Don't you see that?"

"How can you say that? What makes you so sure we're alike? I don't see many similarities between us at all!" she got out tightly, her hazel eyes widening with feminine appeal.

"Only because you don't want to acknowledge them. But you can't deny the physical side of this relationship. At least admit that much!" His fingers tightened on her wrist.

"That's hardly enough, Joel," she pleaded, adding silently: It's not enough to gain my trust; hardly enough to assure myself of your integrity.

"I'll make it enough," he vowed, rising to his feet with sudden purpose and pulling her up beside him. "If it's all I've got to work with at the moment, I'll use it."

Shelley was in his arms before she had a chance to protest, held in bands of velvet-covered steel that made it impossible to retreat before the onslaught of his kiss. He took her mouth with consuming urgency, forcing her lips to part for his sensual invasion.

Hands braced against his shoulders, Shelley managed to wrench her head aside in brief escape. "Joel, no! We have to talk. This isn't the answer!"

"Maybe it is," he growled thickly. "Maybe convincing you that we belong together is like working that damned jigsaw puzzle. I'll take it one section at a time and build on the part you can understand and recognize."

He recaptured her mouth, anchoring her firmly with one hand at the sensitive nape of her neck. Dropping the palm with which he had been cradling her hip, Joel reached around, and without breaking off the kiss, slid the last piece of puzzle into place with a very distinct, very final sounding snap.

Shelley heard the inevitability in the small sound, and her eyes opened in silent protest. He lifted his head a fraction of an inch and stared down at her for a long moment. No words were spoken, but the sense of inevitability engendered by the concluding move of the puzzle game set alight every nerve in Shelley's body.

She did want him, she thought with deep wonder. With all her heart and soul, she wanted him. Never had it been like this. How could she deny herself the warmth and oneness, the excitement and fulfillment, she would find in Joel's arms?

And he wanted her; she could be certain of that. If only she could be as certain that he wasn't also trying to manipulate her for business reasons.

"The puzzle is completed, sweetheart," he groaned

huskily against her throat. "It's time to go to bed." He moved his lips to graze her mouth in a sensuous, persuasive caress.

"Do you always play an honest game?" Shelley couldn't keep herself from asking in a voice that throbbed with emotion and uncertainty.

"I always play by the rules." A small, indulgent smile tugged at the edge of his mouth as he lifted his hand to spear his fingers through her nearly dry hair.

"Whose rules?"

"My own," he replied easily.

Shelley shook her head once. "How can that possibly be fair to me?"

"Because, whether you know it or not, I think you play by the same ones."

"But how can I be sure?" she whispered beseechingly.

"You'll have to trust me for now."

"That's just it, Joel. I don't know you well enough yet to trust you completely. Don't you understand? I want to wait until everything is clear, until I can know for certain—" She broke off helplessly before the blue fire in his eyes and the passionate curve of his mouth.

"I," Joel declared in a voice of thickest satin, "will show you how to approach the problem." He scooped her up into his arms and started down the hall toward her bedroom.

"Oh, Joel . . ." But the whispered sound of his name was an implicit surrender to the moment and the man, and he heard it. She needed him, wanted him in a way she could not yet define or deny.

"You take it one step at a time, honey. You build on the portion you have, the part you know. Just like the jigsaw puzzle. I think you trust me on this level, at least, so this is the level we'll work from."

"But you want more?" she breathed as he set her down in the middle of the bed.

"Yes, I want more."

She watched with luminous eyes as he stripped off his shirt and slung it over the nearest post of her bed. He smiled at her mesmerized stare, and then he leaned down, planting large hands on either side of her body. Shelley looked up at him, wanting him, needing him and knowing it probably showed.

"For the moment, in this room, from now until sunrise, do you trust me, Shelley Banning?" he questioned throatily.

"Yes." It was the truth. Accepting it, Shelley put up her hand to trace tenderly the aggressive line of his jaw. She felt the tremor that went through him at her touch. "Yes, Joel. Tonight, here and now, I trust you."

He leaned farther forward and kissed her heavily, druggingly, and she sensed the relief and, perhaps, thankfulness in him. It dazed her, but before she could respond, he was pulling away reluctantly.

Without a word, he turned and ducked briefly into the bathroom where he had showered earlier. He switched off the light behind him as he came back into the bedroom, but she saw the shaving kit in his hand as he came toward her.

Shelley glanced questioningly from the kit to his smiling, sensual eyes as he set the leather bag on the carved Mediterranean chest beside the bed.

"I brought it in with me earlier when I dropped off the groceries before going out to hunt you down at the pool," he explained calmly.

"Something told you that you might be spending the night?" she said wryly.

"I keep telling you that one of us has to exercise a little foresight and planning." He came down beside her and gathered her against him, the momentary humor fading as smoldering desire turned the steel in his eyes to platinum.

Slowly, caressingly, he began to undress her, finding the buttons of her shirt with fingers that shook ever so slightly. Her own soft hands moved over him with a similar, growing urgency. When her hands fluttered to the fastening of his jeans, gliding lightly over the hardness of his body, Joel groaned words of excitement against her throat and arched himself into her for a moment, forcing her hand more firmly around him.

Then he drew in his lean stomach, inviting her to undo the jeans. She did so, moaning as he opened the front of her shirt and found the fullness of her unconfined breasts.

"I think you must have been made for me," he muttered, showering small hungry kisses across her shoulders and down toward the curving shape of her breasts. "I can lose myself in your body, sweetheart. Soft and warm and—"

"And a bit rounded?" she concluded ruefully, stroking his chest down to his navel but not yet dipping her fingertips into the opening she had made in his jeans.

"Did you know there was a time in my life when I actually thought I liked skinny blondes?" He chuckled warmly, using his thumb to coax forth her nipple.

"But not any longer?" The peak of her breast was tautening deliciously beneath his touch, and Shelley sighed as her body gave itself up to the joy of the moment.

"Not since the day you walked into my shop and asked me for a hundred grand. Now I like rounded, nervy women with hair the color of toast. And there's only one around who seems to fit the description."

"Oh, Joel!"

"Go on touching me, Shelley," he begged hoarsely as she toyed with the tapering auburn hair on his chest. "I want to feel your hands all over me. You have such wonderfully soft hands."

He caught the nipple he had been caressing between

his lips, letting his teeth tease the hard bud as he slid his palms beneath the waistband of her jeans and peeled off the remainder of her clothing. Then he lifted his hips from the bed, and she rapidly removed his clothes as well. When they lay naked together at last, Joel muttered an exclamation of need and captured her wrists gently in a one-handed grip.

Slowly, he lifted his head, his eyes holding hers as he pulled her arms upward. She watched him from beneath heavy lashes as he carefully stretched her body out, trapping her twisting limbs and holding them still. His ankle locked hers, and with one hand he bound her wrists. Then, holding her sensually captive, he began a leisurely exploration of her body with his lips and his free hand.

Trailing his fingers down from her shoulders, he let them rasp teasingly across her full, aching breasts. The sexual taunting, combined with her inability to shift closer to his touch, was incredibly arousing. The flame that was already shimmering in her lower body glowed several degrees hotter as if by magic.

But when she automatically tried to twist free so that she could return the caress, Joel pinned her even more firmly. Then he leaned across to flick each tight nipple with his tongue. Shelley gasped.

His warm, excitingly rough palm swept down below her breasts as he continued to tantalize the hard crests. Further and further he prowled, holding her still beneath the caressing invasion. At the contour of her waist, he drew an imaginary belt and then he encircled the exquisitely vulnerable navel in a buckle. Shelley arched upward, moaning deep in her throat as the fire flamed along her nerve endings.

"Joel?"

"Trust me," he murmured. "Just give yourself up to me and let me make love to you." The tongue that had been dancing around her nipples drew warm, damp patterns down to the curve of her stomach. The hand that had been playing in that region moved on to trace ever-tightening circles on the outside of her thighs, circles that moved to the inside with slow, compelling arousal.

Shelley thought she would go out of her head beneath the exquisite torture. Her hips arched upward with a strength that would not be denied, but Joel denied it regardless, holding her firmly with his heavy leg and a large, gently competent hand.

"Oh!"

Over and over again the small, stifled moans broke from her lips as he deliberately baited and teased and tantalized her senses. When the probing fingers were ready to feather the inside of her thighs, he opened the way for them by pushing his knee between hers.

"Ah, sweetheart," he growled as he found the dampening warmth of her. "You want me; say you want me."

"Oh, Joel! I've never wanted anyone the way I want you! Please, please . . ."

"I will, darling. I will."

But he teased and provoked her body further, executing patterns of intense delight against the very heart of her passion until she thought she would no longer be able to bear it. Shelley felt acutely sensitive to everything about him as he filled her senses. The clean, musky scent of him enticed her nostrils, the hair-rough leg thrown across hers was a primitive chaining that drove her wild, the touch of his hands tantalized every square inch of her skin and the words of sexual promise that he uttered affected her unbelievably.

Joel did not relent in the mastering of her body. He continued to hold her captive while he stoked the fires of her desire. Her legs strained against him, and she twisted with increasing wildness, but there was no escape.

"Joel! Joel, please, I need you!"

He ignored the blatant plea until she was gasping for air and the muscles in her rounded buttocks were tight with the effort to arch into his caress.

"A little longer, sweetheart, a little longer," he crooned.

But Shelley was beyond the soothing reach of his voice. "Damn it, Joel," she bit out, lashes squeezing tightly shut in her passion. "Love me, please love me. Now!" She didn't think about the words. They were the right ones somehow, but she didn't think about them. Tomorrow she would think about what she was really asking.

He kissed the delicate inside of her thigh, his teeth closing gently on the soft flesh, and Shelley cried out once more with unrestrained passion. Then he lifted himself away from her, still using his legs to pin her lower body, and reached into the leather shaving kit for the protection he had assumed as his responsibility.

When he was ready, he released her, preparing to lower himself fully along her length and complete the union. But Shelley had been wound more tautly than any spring. When he temporarily removed his leg from hers and let go of her wrists, she seemed to explode, swarming over him with a force that pushed him down onto his back.

She saw the delighted sensuality in his eyes, heard the groan of wonder and satisfaction that began deep in his chest, but she paid no real heed. She flowed across him, straddling his hips with her own and digging her nails into the smooth muscles of his shoulders in an agony of need.

"Shelley!" He growled her name thickly as he circled her hips with strong hands and pulled her down to join them completely.

Shelley needed no urging. She was wild, totally abandoned, totally caught up in her flaming need for him. When his body thrust upward, surging into hers, she clung to him, her face buried against his sweat-dampened chest, her fingers clenched fiercely.

His hands closed around her rounded bottom and propelled her into the rhythm of his need. She gave herself up to the primitive pattern of the ultimate game because the rhythm satisfied her needs as much as it did his. Together they fit each other like the pieces of the jigsaw puzzle, completing, making whole, creating a satisfying picture only they could experience.

Time seemed to gather itself and then plunge onward toward a bursting escape. Shelley's senses, heightened to a fever pitch by the erotic teasing Joel had subjected them to, were beyond any recall. They were close to an overload status, and when Joel felt the initial convulsion begin to sweep through her body, he doubled the intensity of his driving pattern.

Shelley went violently taut, her nails sharp in the tanned skin they clutched, her head thrown back. The shivering tremors ricocheted back and forth through her body, and somewhere in the middle of the incredible release, she was aware of Joel's cry of masculine surrender and triumph.

"Shelley! My God, Shelley!"

Time, which had been spinning out of control, suddenly stood still. Or perhaps it merely moved on without them. In any event, the two people locked in an embrace on the bed ignored it as they drifted slowly in the aftermath of their passion. The dampness of their still-joined bodies seemed to add somehow to the overwhelming sense of closeness Shelley was experiencing. When she idly touched her fingertips to a tiny rivulet of moisture on Joel's chest, she wondered at the intimacy of the moment.

"You're a woman of power," Joel whispered deeply as she lifted her eyes to meet his. "I feel one moment as if

I've got you in the palm of my hand, and then you overwhelm me."

Gently, reluctantly, Shelley freed herself from his body and snuggled lazily on her side, curling into him. "It was all your fault for teasing me so."

"I used to wonder what would happen at the zoo if one disobeyed the rules about teasing the wild cats." He chuckled. "Now I know."

"Learn anything?"

"Only that I'll have to try it again sometime." He grinned.

She smiled and said nothing, gazing dreamily up at the ceiling.

"Shelley?"

"Mmmm?"

"Still trust me?"

"You said I could until sunrise," she reminded him softly.

"Yes."

"Then what happens?" she asked huskily.

"You keep building on what you have until all the pieces fit." He swung himself off the bed. "Lord, woman, you sure know how to weaken a man!" he added in passionate complaint as he made his way across the room to the bath.

Shelley stared after him. Weaken? Joel Cassidy? She doubted it. He was the one who had held power in this room tonight, bringing her alive beneath his touch, trapping the passion and feeding it until it broke free to engulf them both. She knew she could not deny the fact that he had been with her every step of the way. He made love with total honesty, total involvement. She could trust him tonight.

Shelley found herself telling him that much over and over during the remainder of the night. She gave him her trust until sunrise, freeing herself to give and receive with equal honesty. Again and again Joel rekindled the desire in her and then satisfied it. She knew the triumph and delight in him, but she did not begrudge him those emotions because her own reactions were so in tune with them. Here in this bed with him, she felt safe and protected and warm. She would not worry about sunrise when it came.

It did come eventually, stealing softly into the windows shortly before the alarm clock on the chest beside the bed rattled harshly. Shelley awoke to the noise and the desert dawn, stirring languidly against the lean, muscled shape beside her. One of Joel's large hands emerged from under the sheet to throttle the alarm.

"Do you always get up so early?" he growled.

She grinned wickedly. "Are you always surly in the mornings?" His tousled red hair invited her touch, but she withheld it as he turned his head on the pillow to face her. "I'm like you. Once I'm fed, I'm fine."

"Don't remind me! I've eaten more during the past few days than I have for a month. It's going to start showing soon, I'm afraid."

He ran a proprietary hand down the curve of her hip and shook his head with grave certainty. "We'll make sure you work it off. In any event, I told you I've decided I like my women nicely rounded now."

She found herself believing the teasing words. He *did* like her shape, she thought with pleasure. That made her feel good. She threw back the gold and white striped sheets and bounced cheerfully out of bed. "Onward and upward. The day has begun," she announced, reaching for a persimmon-colored robe as he watched her with lazy indulgence. When she finished tying the sash around her waist, her eyes lifted to meet the possessive gaze he was aiming at her, and Shelley felt a wave of deep shyness go through her. She knew there was red staining

over heels for a man who should never have been allowed to become more than a business associate, and probably not even that if she'd been really intelligent about the matter!

Last night she had given him her trust until dawn. She had felt safe during the night, sure of her decision. Now sunrise had brought a new day, and she had to think. She had to decide how much more trust she could add to the measure he had demanded from her during the hours of darkness. A little piece at a time—that was the way you put together a puzzle. You built on the part you knew, and she knew she could trust him as a lover.

Taking a deep, steadying breath, Shelley shoved open the car door and headed for the main entrance to her office building. Deciding how far one could trust a lover wasn't the only puzzle that was put together a piece at a time.

The same principle could be used in business.

Helping herself to a cup of coffee from the pot Carol had already started, Shelley made her way to her office and sat down to stare at the top of her desk, her brow knitted in thought.

Sometimes after one started a puzzle, it was useful to back off and come at it from another angle. Had she been taking the wrong angle on the threat to Ackerly Manufacturing?

What if Joel were being totally honest with her? What if he had no manipulative schemes for Ackerly other than getting back his hundred thousand dollars with interest? What other possibilities opened up if one went on that assumption? How else could that phone call be explained? Why else would someone wish to "compensate" her for dumping Ackerly Manufacturing as a client?

The questions spun around through her head, gnawing, meshing, raising further questions. There was another possible reason for a phone call such as the one she had received; another reason why someone would wish her to remove herself from the Ackerly picture.

If one assumed Joel's innocence, then someone else entirely had instigated that phone call, perhaps implicating Joel deliberately to put her off the track.

Shelley's nail tapped the polished desk thoughtfully, forcing herself to examine the new possibility from all sides. Yes, it was an angle that should be thoroughly checked out.

And if it checked out, Joel would be in the clear. She would be able to trust him completely.

Shelley reached for the phone and dialed Dean Ackerly's number.

8

At five-thirty that evening, Shelley sat in a shadowy booth watching the posh bar fill with the lively after-work crowd that patronized it. It was "happy hour," and the drinks were half price. A huge buffet had been set out to entice the work-weary singles. Shelley had a few doubts as to how many were technically "single," but that was par for the course. It was a polished, leather-and-wood and hanging-green-plants sort of place, and the people filling it were definitely upwardly mobile: stockbrokers, young corporation types, advertising people. All well dressed, trendy and exuding a self-confidence that didn't quite mask the underlying air of desperation. The goal of being here this evening was, after all, to attract a mate. Preferably one who wouldn't make a nuisance of himself or herself by clinging in the morning.

Shelley absently stirred the margarita she had poured from the pitcher on the table and watched the swinging glass doors expectantly. She saw Dean Ackerly as he walked through a moment later, scanning the room for her. Lifting a hand to silently signal her location, Shelley took a sip of the margarita and watched him stride toward her through the laughing, boisterous crowd. A good-looking man, a man who could handle the swinging scene around him or enjoy the ballet, a man who, with a bit of help from her, would make a success out of Ackerly Manufacturing. But even as she watched him slide into the leather seat across from her, she knew that she would never be able to find with him what she was finding with Joel Cassidy. Proving Joel's innocence would be the most important job she had ever tackled. Her own heart was at stake.

"I had no idea accountants hung out in places like this," Dean teased as he helped himself from the margarita pitcher. "You surprise me."

"Sorry, I can't claim I chose the place from personal experience. I saw a James Bond movie once where the contact meeting between two agents was conducted in a noisy bar. I stole the idea, I'm afraid."

"Well, it would be a good bet this place isn't bugged," he agreed. "But then, neither is my office. Or yours, for that matter!" He chuckled, glancing around to eye a blonde at the buffet table appreciatively. "Hungry?" he added, turning back.

"No, thanks," Shelley said automatically. It crossed her mind fleetingly that Joel wouldn't have accepted her refusal. Dean did.

"Mind if I run over and get some potato skins and fried chicken wings?"

"No, of course not."

She watched him move to the buffet table and say a

few words to the blonde as he helped himself from several chafing dishes. A charming smile, she thought inconsequentially, and it was having its effect on the blonde, who bubbled enthusiastically. But Dean's smile lacked that element of boyish wickedness that Joel's had, and it lacked the slightly crooked tooth, too. Dean's teeth were quite perfect.

"Okay, Agent X," Dean declared as he resumed his seat with a full plate, "let's have the message that is so important it has to be passed in surroundings where neither of us will be overheard or interrupted."

"You want the good news first or the bad news?"

He winced. "How bad is the bad?"

"Could be bad enough to account for Ackerly Manufacturing's slide toward bankruptcy," Shelley told him flatly.

"You're kidding!" Dean put down the fried chicken wing in his hand and stared at her. "What's going on, Shelley? Why the mysterious phone call this morning and all this secrecy?"

She took a breath and plunged in. "Dean, I want a full investigative audit of Ackerly's books, and I want it done with my own team from Mason Wells. I want to walk into Ackerly's offices first thing in the morning without any warning by you to any member of your staff, and I want *all* the books."

His eyes narrowed as he watched her, stunned. "You're talking about looking for embezzlement?"

"Bribes, kickbacks, embezzlement, payoffs, I don't know what I'm looking for, but whatever it is, it's enough to make someone offer me a bribe to dump Ackerly as a client!"

"A bribe!"

Shelley nodded grimly. "My first assumption was that it had something to do with that loan from Cassidy. His name was mentioned," she admitted. "But now I have a feeling it could be totally unrelated and that someone is using the Cassidy mess as a red herring. That someone would have to be high up in your management staff in order to know about Cassidy and the land deal in the first place."

Dean took a large gulp of his margarita as he considered the news. His grip on the stem of the glass was rather fierce. "What makes you think it isn't related to the Cassidy loan?"

This was it. How did you tell a business client that you were falling in love with a man and therefore couldn't bear to believe him guilty of such conniving and manipulative behavior? Dean would probably dump *her* as his consulting accountant if she said she trusted Joel Cassidy as a lover and therefore wanted to trust him in every other area of life!

"It's too obvious, for one thing. The person who called me to offer the bribe used his name and deliberately made me think that Joel was behind it. Frankly, the man is too damn smart to approach the matter in such a heavy-handed fashion. I think he'd be a lot more subtle about it." Subtle enough to seduce the accountant in charge of saving Ackerly and gain her trust and confidence that way? Shelley pushed the thought aside. She did not want to believe him guilty. She *wouldn't* believe him guilty!

"You have a point about that," Dean said grudgingly.

"There's another thing," Shelley pursued determinedly. "If there's something really big in those books, it could account for a lot of the trouble that Ackerly's found itself in during the past eighteen months."

"You think kickbacks or payoffs could add up to enough to actually push the company toward bankruptcy?" Dean looked startled.

She nodded. "It's happened before. There are cases where that kind of thing has cost a company literally millions! But it could be another kind of scam altogether. It could be a deliberate effort to bleed off as much money as possible for as long as possible until the company goes into bankruptcy."

"Embezzlement?"

She shrugged. "I don't know, Dean, but I want those books, and I want them without any warning to anyone. Will you give me permission to do it?"

"Sure, you're the accountant, but haven't you already been through the books enough to have noticed if something were wrong?" he asked quizzically.

Shelley shook her head. "It's not that simple. I've been approaching the company records from an entirely different angle. Looking for ways to cut back, consolidate, tighten up. I haven't been looking for criminal activity. That takes a full-scale investigative audit. I'll be going into the computerized records, too."

Dean whistled soundlessly and took another sip of his drink. "I get the feeling tomorrow is going to be a big day in the Ackerly accounting department!"

"I'll bring a team in at seven-thirty in the morning. That's a half an hour before your staff arrives. We'll be on the scene and have the records we need before anyone realizes what's happening."

"Sounds like a military operation!"

"It'll look a little like one, too!" Shelley smiled wryly. "But if we find evidence of a scam, it would sure explain a lot of Ackerly's problems."

"You mean I wouldn't have to wonder how my father suddenly became such a poor executive? I have thought about that from time to time. I told myself that it happens to the best of managers and that he was getting old, but I *have* wondered how the slide really got started." He broke off and gave her a hard glance. "But you're sure it's got nothing to do with the Cassidy deal?"

"I can't be absolutely *sure* of anything, Dean. I only know that the bribe just didn't strike me as being his style." She tried to make it sound very positive, very certain. It was important to convince Dean that the audit was necessary and that Joel might be innocent of any wrongdoing. She couldn't abide the thought that Joel might have been behind that bribe and that he might be angling to let Ackerly slip into bankruptcy.

"You could be right," Dean said slowly, and then nodded firmly. "Okay. I'll be at the office at seven-thirty tomorrow morning, and I'll let you into the accounting department. Is your team ready to go?"

"Yes, I lined it up late this afternoon. I was hoping you'd agree that the audit was necessary."

"If you can't trust your accountant, who can you trust?" he murmured. He reached for the margarita pitcher and poured another glass for her. "Come on, Shelley, show me on paper what you'll actually be doing tomorrow."

Shelley glanced at her watch. "Maybe I'd better see if there are any carrot sticks left at the buffet table," she said with an air of resignation. "It's getting late, and this will take awhile."

Two hours, one margarita and several carrot sticks later, Shelley bade good night to her client, who was still shaking his head trying to imagine who in his organization was out to destroy the firm, and climbed into her car for the drive back home. She had what she wanted from Dean, a shot at proving Joel's innocence and a chance to discover if there was more to Ackerly's financial woes than initially met the eye. Shelley was satisfied with the night's work.

Her mind was spinning with plans as she pulled into

the drive and parked her car, spinning so fast, in fact, that she didn't see the white Maserati at the curb until she was heading up the walk toward her front door. When she bent over to search for the right key beneath the glow of the light, she saw it out of the corner of her eye.

Joel was waiting for her! The realization brought a small chill of uncertainty. She had wanted to wait until the audit had started before she confronted him again; wanted to wait until she had some indication that her trust was not misplaced. But he was here, waiting for her. Shelley bit her lip and thought fleetingly of simply getting back into her car and disappearing until the following evening. Everything would be so much simpler if she just had a little time to be *sure*.

Well, she would just have to play the game a while longer, Shelley instructed herself resolutely as she inserted the key in the lock. When this was all over, she would be able to face Joel and tell him that she really did trust him. For tonight, however, she would be as she was last night—wary but sure that she could at least trust him until morning.

The door opened easily, and she realized it hadn't been locked. Where was the man she knew was waiting? Shelley blinked in the darkness of the hallway and groped for the light switch. She had not seen him in the car, so he must be somewhere in the house. Why were all the lights turned off? A wave of unease swept through her as she stepped into the living room.

"Hello, Shelley. It's about time you got home."

There was barely any satin at all left in the soft voice that greeted her as she came to a halt at the entrance to the living room. His tone betrayed fiercely suppressed anger.

"Hello, Joel."

She could make him out now in the faint glow of

moonlight coming through the patio window. He was seated in the dark-leather recliner to her right, and as she watched, fascinated, he lifted his hand to take a sip from the glass he was holding. She could not see the blueness of his eyes in the darkness, but the steel seemed very apparent. The sense of unease she had experienced earlier grew by several quantum leaps.

"You're late," he observed simply.

"I didn't know you would be waiting for me," she tried to say calmly, taking a step forward to drop her shoulder bag on a convenient table. As soon as she set the purse down, she regretted it. Her hands suddenly seemed very empty and awkward. What in the world was the matter with her?

"Didn't you?" There was cool mockery in his voice, but it didn't hide the simmering anger. "Didn't you guess I might be waiting, Shelley?"

And now Shelley knew why she felt not only uneasy but downright frightened. The room was permeated with a sense of controlled fury. How much longer would it remain under control?

"No," she tried to say firmly, moving forward to switch on another light in the hope that the illumination would remove some of her nervousness. Her palms, she realized as she flipped the switch, were damp. How strange. "I didn't know you would be waiting. I was working late."

"Not at Mason Wells, you weren't. I called there shortly before five-thirty and was told you'd left for the day."

Shelley swallowed and wished she hadn't had the second margarita. Something told her that in this mood Joel needed very careful handling. With a determinedly relaxed air, she unbuttoned the jacket of the red suit she was wearing and slipped it off. Then she kicked off the red and white pumps and headed for the kitchen in an imitation of her normal after-work behavior.

"Have you eaten?" she asked, opening the refrigerator door.

"I'm not hungry," he said quietly from directly behind her.

She whirled, slamming the refrigerator shut as she realized he'd followed her silently into the kitchen. In the bright glow of the overhead fixture there was no problem at all in making out the color of his eyes. They were the shade of an arctic sea, cold and lethal. The coiled tension in his body promised the menace she had always guessed lurked beneath the surface of the man. Why was he confronting her with it tonight?

"I take it you're a little upset over something?" she hazarded dryly, striving to maintain a casual appearance as she desperately tried to think of something constructive to do. A half-empty bottle of Pinot Noir stood on the counter, and she reached for it and a glass as if for a life line. She didn't particularly want another drink, but she very badly wanted to keep her hands busy so that the trembling in her fingers wouldn't be so noticeable.

"Where were you this evening, Shelley?" he asked flatly, watching her the way she imagined a predator watched a potential victim.

"I told you. I was working."

"Where?"

"What is this? An inquisition? Joel, I have a career that sometimes demands extra time and extra work!"

"It's nearly eight o'clock, and you haven't been working late at the office," he rasped. "Where have you been working, Shelley?"

"Oh, for God's sake!" she exploded in a combination of anger and resentment. All she'd wanted was a little time, and here Joel was pushing her! "You're not my husband, Joel. What right do you have to question my every move? You never made any arrangements this evening for us that I was aware of. It's not as if I'm late for a date or stood you up for someone else!" She gulped the wine in her hand and immediately wished she hadn't. She put the glass down on the tiled counter and leaned back against the cool edge, facing him defiantly.

"Were you with Ackerly?" he demanded harshly.

Her eyes widened at the accuracy of his guess. "As a matter of fact, I was. We were working on his company's problem."

"Where were you working on this 'problem'?" he persisted relentlessly.

"Joel . . . !"

"*Where?*" He didn't raise his voice, but the command in it came through very clearly. Shelley knew with sudden intuition that she wasn't going to escape from the kitchen until he had his answer. She began to feel cornered.

"At a bar downtown," she shot back recklessly, bracing herself with a hand planted on either side of her against the counter. "A *singles* bar."

"Don't look at me that way, Shelley," he warned very softly.

"What way?"

"As if you're defying me to make something of that last statement. Don't challenge me over an issue like this, honey," he advised coolly. "You'll lose. I guarantee it. Now tell me why you met Ackerly in a bar after work and stayed with him for over two hours."

The sense of recklessness, of being pushed when she didn't want to be pushed and of downright resentment grew. Shelley wasn't used to being questioned about her actions, especially by a man. Her hazel eyes narrowed, and flecks of gold swirled in the green and blue depths.

"I've told you that I was working. If you don't like the explanation, I suggest you make up one of your own that you like better."

"You're going to tell me you've spent the past two hours in a bar with a man and that it was strictly business?" he bit out.

"Yes!"

He stared at her for a long moment, and then he seemed to draw a deep breath. "All right." He turned and walked out of the kitchen.

It was Shelley's turn to stare after his retreating figure. "All right!" she repeated dazedly. "Joel, what the hell do you mean, *all right?*" She pushed herself away from the counter and started after him. He was sinking back into the recliner, stretching his feet out as if he intended to stay a while. She stood in front of him with her hands on her hips and glared down at him. One red brow arched questioningly as he looked back at her.

"I said all right because I meant all right. I don't like it; I think you ought to start getting in the habit of working regular hours and not conducting business in bars, but tonight it's all right."

"You mean you've decided to believe me?" she asked, taken aback. She had been psyching herself up for a major battle, and he suddenly wasn't going to fight.

"I believe you." He closed his eyes for a few seconds, and when he opened them again, his gaze was very deep and steady. "But I'd like your word that you will not do much business in that fashion in the future. Why did you have to meet him in a bar after work, Shelley? Why couldn't you have gone to his office during normal hours?"

Shelley sank into the chair across from him, the tension within her fading somewhat as she acknowledged that there wasn't going to be a knock-down, drag-out war over the issue. Joel believed her. He didn't like it, but he believed her.

"I didn't want anyone at Ackerly Manufacturing except

Dean to know what I was planning to do tomorrow," she found herself saying quietly. She looked away from him, out into the darkened patio beyond the sliding-glass door. "I was afraid that if I went to his office or he came to mine, someone would notice the unscheduled meeting and start putting two and two together."

"Why should someone have been more suspicious of this meeting than any other you've had with Ackerly?" Joel asked quietly, his eyes on her profile.

"I just didn't want to take the chance of someone guessing that I . . . Ever since . . ."

"Ever since what?" he prompted as she floundered.

"Joel, I don't want to talk about this," she whispered with unexpected pleading in her voice as she turned her head sharply to meet his gaze. "It really is business, Ackerly business, and I would rather not discuss it."

"Ackerly business is also my business these days, or have you forgotten our agreement? I was to be kept informed at every step along the way, remember?" he retorted coolly.

"I know, but this is—this is different, Joel!"

"Does it affect Ackerly operations? Does it have any bearing on the future of the company? Any impact on the loan I made to the firm?"

The sense of feeling cornered began to return. Shelley looked at him with a desperate kind of helplessness. "Yes! No! Perhaps. Joel, I don't know yet. I need some time!"

"Time to do what?"

"Damn it! Don't push me! I've told you this is business!"

"My business," he emphasized, shoving down the foot rest of the recliner and sitting forward to pin her with a hard expression. "What's going on, Shelley? What are you up to?"

"I thought you said you trusted me," she hedged unhappily.

"I do. That does not mean I don't want to know what's going on!" he shot back implacably.

"I'll tell you when it's all over. If everything works out, I'll give you a full report," she promised hopefully.

"You'll tell me now, sweetheart," he declared forcibly.

"I can't!"

"Why not?" he countered ruthlessly.

"Because it concerns you!" she blazed in a burst of frustrated anger.

"Me!" he repeated, looking thunderstruck. "Shelley, what the hell is going on?"

"Joel, please, just give me a little time," she began earnestly, eyes wide with the appeal she was making.

"Time for what, damn it?" He wasn't going to give up now, and Shelley knew it.

"Time to prove your innocence!" she gritted fiercely, surging to her feet and pacing across the carpet in her stockinged feet. She got as far as the puzzle table before she turned at bay and confronted him. He was on his feet, standing beside the chair with his hands in the back pockets of his jeans. His legs were slightly apart as if he were bracing himself for a fight, and the stern glare with which he searched her face was enough to make the air conditioning superfluous.

"My innocence," he repeated almost neutrally. Shelley didn't trust the tone at all.

"That's all I can say at the moment, Joel."

"The hell it is."

"I promise that I'll explain everything as soon as—"

"You'll explain it now, Shelley."

She shivered. He meant it, and she knew he meant it. Now what was she going to do? A little time. That was all she had wanted, just enough time to make certain. Her eyes closed briefly in silent despair. "Couldn't you trust me just a bit longer, Joel?"

"Trusting you is not the problem," he growled, starting forward slowly. "The problem now seems to be your trust in me. Or rather the lack of it," he concluded emphatically.

Shelley backed away warily as he closed the distance between them. "By tomorrow night I should have a fairly good idea," she began urgently.

"A fairly good idea of whether or not you can trust me? Is that what you're about to say?" He was close; much too close. Shelley backed away another step.

"Joel, I'm doing this for you!"

"What, exactly, are you doing for me?" he asked quietly. He stopped at the puzzle table, and she halted her retreat.

There wasn't much point in trying to stall him any longer, Shelley told herself. He meant to have answers tonight, and he wouldn't let go until he got them. She knew that with the same certainty that she knew the classic accounting equations.

"All right!" she spit out tightly. "I'll tell you what I'm doing for you! I'm descending on Ackerly Manufacturing tomorrow morning with a team of trained auditors! I'm going to take those books apart until I can prove that someone besides you would have a reason to bribe me to get rid of Ackerly as a client. There! Are you satisfied?"

"Bribe you!" He looked genuinely blank. "Who tried to bribe you?"

"If I knew that, I wouldn't have to charge Ackerly's account for a full-scale investigative audit, would I?" she snapped vengefully.

"But who offered it? How was it done? In person?" He rattled off the questions like a machine gun.

"Over the phone." Shelley hugged her arms to herself

and walked away from him to stand in front of the window gazing out into the night. "A woman's voice. She mentioned your name."

Joel swore softly, something harsh and violent. "This person implicated me as the source of the bribe?"

"Yes."

"But why? What reason would I have to do such a thing?" he growled.

She'd gone this far; she might as well tell him everything. "There's a little matter of the land you're holding as collateral on the Ackerly loan being worth five times as much as the loan itself to a certain California real estate conglomerate." Shelley stared very hard into the night, willing him to come back with a demand for another explanation or a dumbfounded denial of any knowledge of the California group's interest in the land. Please, she begged silently, please tell me you know nothing about the true value of that land! In that moment, she knew she would willingly trade her certified public accountant's license for a denial from him.

"Oh, that business," he said dismissively.

Shelley froze. Then she flung herself around to face him, the pain in her clearly reflected in the taut line of her mouth and in the depths of her eyes.

"Joel—Joel, are you telling me you know about the value of that land?" Her voice was a strained whisper, an agonized thread of sound.

He stood where he was, his hands still shoved into his back pockets. "Sure I know about it. Or, to be more precise, I've heard the rumors about it. I haven't actually discussed it with anyone in that group of investors."

"You know the land Phil Ackerly used to secure the loan from you is worth half a million dollars?" she got out weakly.

"Yeah. What about it?"

"What about it!" she exclaimed. "How can you ask me that? Joel, did you have someone call me up and offer me a bribe to stay out of Ackerly affairs?"

"No."

Shelley faltered uncertainty under the impact of the quiet denial. In spite of herself, a fierce flicker of hope sprang back to life before it had even been fully extinguished. "But you know about the potential value of the land?"

"Yup."

His laconic drawl irritated her. "You knew about it, but you weren't going to act on the information? You weren't hoping Ackerly would go into bankruptcy and you'd get the land?" she asked quickly.

"After Phil died, I didn't feel any sentimental attachment to Ackerly Manufacturing, Shelley," he stated deliberately. "If the company had gone under and I'd taken possession of the property, it wouldn't have kept me awake nights."

"Oh," she whispered forlornly.

"At least that's how I felt about the situation until you came on the scene," he went on coolly. "Within half an hour of talking to you, I found myself agreeing to extend the loan and let you have your chance to save the firm. Or don't you remember that?"

"Of course I do," she said breathlessly. "I kept telling myself you would never have agreed to do that if you weren't willing to give me my chance with Ackerly."

"Did you?" he asked skeptically.

"Yes. Oh, Joel, this is all so confusing!"

"There's nothing confusing about it. We made a bargain, you and I, and I've stuck to my end of it."

She sighed and turned back toward the window. "I—I was terrified you might have seduced me as a way of controlling the bargain."

"I was a little nervous at first that you were doing the

same thing to me," he admitted quietly. "It occurred to me you might have slept with me in order to keep me under your control while you dealt with Ackerly's financial problems. What better way to keep the most difficult creditor at bay than to keep him happy in bed?"

"Don't say that," she begged. "I never planned any such thing!"

"I knew that after the first night, Shelley," Joel told her calmly. She felt rather than heard him move toward her across the deep-champagne-colored carpet. Her body stiffened as he came up behind her, but he didn't touch her. "I wanted you from the first time I saw you, but I trusted you after the first time I made love to you. I keep telling you we're a lot alike."

"Thank you, Joel. For trusting me, I mean," she whispered tremulously. "I had no idea you were wondering about my motives. I'll be so glad when this audit is over and everything is out in the open."

There was a silence behind her. Then Joel asked deliberately, "Do you trust me, Shelley?"

"I—I think so," she managed carefully. "It's like you said. One builds trust bit by bit, like the jigsaw puzzle. A piece at a time. In a couple of days I'll have the answers to the questions I have about the Ackerly books . . . and another piece of the puzzle." She turned around to stare searchingly up at him. "When this is all over, we can start with a clean slate, can't we, Joel? We'll both be sure of each other's motives, and we'll know where we stand."

"No."

"What do you mean?"

"I mean we can't start over after you've satisfied yourself about my innocence," he stated evenly. "I mean that I want from you the same thing I'm prepared to give: unequivocal trust. No reservations and no waiting for proof. And I want it tonight, Shelley."

"Joel! You said yourself that trust is something one builds slowly!"

"I've changed my mind," he announced flatly. "I want you to do more than trust me, Shelley Banning. I want you to have complete faith in me even if you don't have all the proof you need to show I'm not trying to manipulate an Ackerly bankruptcy or gain that chunk of land. I want you to say you'll come and live with me, and nothing which comes to light during your audit will make any difference. I want you to take my word for the fact that I've played the game straight with you, and I want all that before you even begin your damn audit!"

"Please, Joel, you're asking too much, too soon! I just need a little time!" Shelley pleaded.

"Sorry, I'm not making any more loans tonight. Not of time or money or anything else. I'm demanding payment in full!"

"Payment for what?" she rasped, beginning to grow angry under the implacability of his new mood. "I don't owe you anything, Joel Cassidy!"

"Perhaps 'payment' was the wrong word," he agreed ruthlessly. "What I want from you is more in the nature of a gift, isn't it? A gift of trust and—"

She stared at him open-mouthed as he cut off his demands in midflow. "Trust and what else, Joel?" she snapped, goaded.

"Figure it out for yourself," he tossed back, spinning around on one booted heel and heading for the door. "And when you do, come and tell me about it."

"Joel, come back here! Where the hell do you think you're going?" she blazed at his back. He was almost at the door.

"Out. It's been a while since I did some socializing with my customers!"

"Is that a way of saying you're going to go out and get drunk in one of your tavern locations?" she hissed furiously. How dare he walk out on her like this?

"At least you'll know where to find me if you want me, won't you?"

The door slammed shut behind him.

9

——⚭⚭⚭⚭⚭⚭⚭⚭——

How did he dare walk out on her at a time like this? Walk out to go drinking in some damn tavern, no less?

Shelley stood staring speechlessly at the closed door as the Maserati roared off into the night. When her vocal powers finally returned, they seemed extremely limited for a time, consisting of a small, ancient variety of expressions angry women have used to describe the male of the species since time immemorial.

"Who the hell do you think you are?" she finally concluded, hurling the accusation at the silent door. "Just who the hell do you think you are, Joel Cassidy?"

When the door refused to answer, Shelley began to pace the room, her nylon-sheathed feet silent on the carpet as she wove a restless pattern. What right did he have to issue demands and then take himself off to get drunk in some sleazy bar? What right did he have to walk out on her in the middle of an extremely crucial discussion?

All she had wanted was some time, she told herself in angry frustration. Some time to establish his innocence beyond a doubt. Was that too much to ask? He could have given her that much, surely? After all she'd been through lately, it was hardly asking too much of him!

He wanted her trust, did he? Hadn't she virtually declared her belief in him already? What other logical, reasonable, sane accountant would have gone looking for another culprit on whom to blame Ackerly's troubles when the evidence pointed to an obvious suspect? Didn't he understand how much trust she'd already placed in him? How she was going to do everything possible to prove he hadn't tried to manipulate the Ackerly deal? And she was still going to do that even though Joel had admitted he knew about the California conglomerate's interest in the land!

"Damn!" Shelley's small, curled fist struck the edge of the table as she paced past it. No, Joel was no longer willing to give her any time. He wanted everything, and he wanted it tonight!

"What do you think you're doing to me?" she muttered softly as she came to a halt beside the puzzle table. She stood staring down at the scene of Venice. "What in hell do you think you're doing to me?"

He wanted a commitment from her, a commitment based solely on a woman's instinctive trust, not on proof of his innocence.

Staring sightlessly at the canals in the puzzle, Shelley tried to sort through her emotions. As she did so, some of the red-hot anger faded. When all was said and done, one fact emerged clearly: she was in love with the man. Even through her rage she could acknowledge that much. She was in love with him, and he was demanding a declaration of unequivocal trust.

Joel had no right to ask that at this point, Shelley told herself wildly. But hadn't he given it to her? There was no doubt in her mind that he'd been in a fury tonight when she'd walked through the door. But he'd accepted her explanation, slim as it was. He hadn't liked it, had made it clear he didn't want the incident to be repeated, but he'd *believed* it. Without any proof. And she knew with feminine intuition that Joel Cassidy was a very possessive man. It had been asking a lot of him to expect him to believe she'd been working this evening.

Deep down, what did that same feminine intuition tell her about her faith in him? Didn't she believe in him?

"Of course I do!" she growled to the room at large. "Why else would I be going through all this trouble?" As an accountant, she was trained to see all the facts as they were set down in dollars and cents. Automatically, she had set out to get them down in just such a fashion in order to clear Joel.

But did she really need that to satisfy her own heart? Perhaps, to satisfy Ackerly management, she would need those facts and figures, but were they truly necessary to satisfy herself?

"Joel Cassidy, so help me, when I get my hands on you—" The sentence died on her lips as she reached for the phone book with abrupt decision. She would find that man tonight and tell him exactly what she thought of him.

And then she would give him her heart and her trust, because there really was no choice. Tonight she must play the game his way and believe him when he said he always played by the rules, even if those rules were his own.

The number for Cassidy & Co. was listed under "Amusement Devices" in the yellow pages. She dialed it with a sense of grim determination.

"I'm trying to reach Mr. Cassidy," she announced to the answering-service operator who took the call.

"I'm sorry, Mr. Cassidy is not in at the moment. I can have one of the company's service people return your call," the woman on the other end of the line offered helpfully. "Or I could take a message and give it to Mr. Cassidy when he phones in for messages."

"When is he likely to do that?" Shelley questioned in irritation.

"Probably not until tomorrow," the woman hazarded honestly.

"I see. Well, in that case, will you please have one of the service people call this number?" She gave her phone number quickly and hung up. Fuming with impatience, Shelley sat by the phone until it rang shrilly a few minutes later. She grabbed the receiver on the first ring.

"Mac Swanson here. What can I do for you?" inquired a cheerful male voice. Shelley could hear a television set in the background and the chatter of children. Mac Swanson was apparently a family man.

"Mr. Swanson, you don't know me, but I'm trying to track down Joel Cassidy this evening. I believe he's making a, uh, tour of some of his tavern locations tonight, and I was wondering if you might have some idea where I could reach him?"

"You Shelley Banning?" Mac Swanson interrupted with great interest.

"Why, yes, as a matter of fact, I am. How did you know?" she asked in astonishment.

"Just had a call from Joel a few minutes ago. He said you might be getting in touch. I've got some addresses to give you."

"Addresses?" Shelley demanded suspiciously. "Plural?"

"Yeah. You want to copy them down? It's a list of some bars and taverns where we've got machines."

"But which one was he calling from?" Shelley pressed anxiously.

"Can't say. Kind of a quick call. You want these addresses?"

Shelley stifled a groan of dismay. "Yes, please," she said meekly, reaching for a pencil and paper. Dutifully, she copied down the list as he read it off.

"There, that's the lot," he announced helpfully. Then he asked in a tone of deeply amused curiosity, "What are you going to do when you find him?"

"Throttle him." Shelley hung up the phone and sat glaring at the hastily scribbled list. Joel was playing games again. They were going to engage in a game of hide-and-seek through some of the sleaziest taverns in town, places she normally wouldn't have set foot in escorted, much less alone!

Grimly, she got to her feet and headed for the bedroom to change into a pair of jeans and a long-sleeved shirt in rich, royal purple. Then, remembering some of the places she would be visiting, she reached for the cuffed suede boots at the back of the closet.

"I ought to be buckling on a holster. This is beginning to feel like *High Noon*," she grumbled to herself in the mirror. Then she headed for her car.

There was no way of knowing where she would find Joel, so the only logical thing to do was choose the address of the tavern nearest to her and start there. Twenty minutes later, Shelley parked her neat little car in a parking lot full of battered pickup trucks and viewed the first stop on her list with dismay.

There were no windows, but the door under the flashing neon sign stood open to the desert night, and the blaring music from the juke box poured forth. It was a guitar-oriented country-western song about drinking and loving, and it seemed to suit the clientele. Shelley watched the pair of cowboys who were entering the place and grimaced. Scuffed boots, worn jeans and crisp white shirts. The tavern was going to be filled with a lot more just like them, and none of them were going to be fake. This sort of place catered to the real thing in cowboys and truckers.

Well, she wasn't going to get anywhere hiding in the car. Summoning up her nerve and a large measure of her annoyance with Joel, Shelley opened the door and climbed out.

She was accosted the minute she stepped through the door. A callused palm slapped the curve of her hip, and Shelley spun around to glare at a grinning young man with a western hat pushed back on his curling black hair.

"Buy you a beer, honey?" he offered expectantly.

Shelley took a savage grip on her temper and reined it in with an effort. "No, thanks. I'm looking for someone." She had to say it rather loudly in order to make herself heard over the sound of the juke box and the beeps, crashes and explosions from the array of pinball and video games along one wall.

"You just found someone, honey. Me. Come on and I'll get you a drink." The young man took hold of her arm and began steering her in the direction of the bar. Shelley dug in her heels.

"I said I was looking for someone. Someone in particular," she said firmly. "Please let me go."

"Now, honey, there ain't no call to get unfriendly," he protested. "I only want to buy you a beer and maybe talk for a while." He grinned innocently again, and Shelley thought about kneeing him in the groin. Exactly what she needed. A bar brawl with herself as one of the main contestants. Damn Joel! She was going to strangle him for this!

"Look, if you don't let go of my arm—" she began

firmly, only to be interrupted by the bartender, who had emerged from behind the bar to approach the other two. He wiped his hands on his apron as he walked.

"You Shelley Banning by any chance?" he asked politely. He was a large man with a beer belly and a friendly, graying mustache. He obviously had the respect of his patrons because the young cowboy dropped her arm as the older man slid him a stern glance.

"Yes, I am. I'm looking for Joel Cassidy. Is he here?"

The bartender grinned as the young man morosely took himself off without a word. "Said to tell you to have a look around and see. I'm supposed to make sure you do your looking without any interference." He nodded toward the amusement machines lined up against the far wall. Through the smoky haze a chorus line of jeaned men and a few women moved in strange, tightly woven little dances as they used body English to urge a winning game out of their chosen machines. "You just put up a hand and holler if anyone bothers you, okay?"

"Thanks," Shelley muttered dryly. Clearly, Joel had left instructions as to how the game was to be played. But though she was the chief player, she was only going to get a peek at the rules as she went along. Her mouth tight, she shoved her hands in her pockets and started toward the row of pinball wizards and video-game tacticians.

The glow of the game lights revealed each player in turn as she walked down the row. There wasn't a redhead among them. She stood watching in fascination for a moment after she'd finished her initial survey. Several masculine heads turned interestedly in her direction, and there were several offers to buy her a beer, but Shelley shook her head in firm denial, glanced toward the bar where the big man watched helpfully and then turned around and walked out. The lingering glance of the young, black-haired cowboy followed her out the door.

Shelley got into her car with a sense of relief that lasted only as long as it took to drive to the next tavern on her list. Here the parking lot seemed filled with bigger and more battered pickup trucks, and there were a few large semis at the rear. This time the man behind the bar, a tall, thin, balding person with rather wide shoulders, came forward before any of the patrons could get off their bar stools.

"You Shelley Banning?" he asked politely, dark eyes expectant.

"Yes, I am." She smiled with wry humor. "You're supposed to make sure I have a chance to look around in peace, right?"

"That's right, ma'am. Phone call from Joel a while back. Help yourself," he added, nodding toward the smoke-filled room. "Yell good and loud if you need me."

There was a live band in this place; a woman with long blonde hair and a skin-tight silver lamé jumpsuit done in a western style sang throatily into the mike, backed up by a surprisingly good group of musicians. They had to work hard to be heard over the clatter of amusement games at the far end of the room.

Shelley made her way through the crowd, ignoring the occasional pat on her derrière and the inviting grins on several male faces. Once again, she surveyed the video game and pinball players in the bright glow of the machine lights. No redheaded, blue-eyed man among them.

The contestants draped themselves in various postures over the machines, setting down the beers in their hands to grasp the little joy sticks that controlled the action on the screens. Faces contorted in grimaces of urgent excitement, laughter and sometimes frustration as waves of invaders were fought off or little cartoon characters ran around gobbling up dots.

"Hey there, little lady, want to play a game?" One of the players turned to leer at her as he finished his game. He was perhaps forty, married, she was sure, and looking for some action. She glanced at the video screen behind him as he lounged on the control panel.

"No, thanks. I'm just looking for someone."

"I'll help you look." He chuckled, straightening to move toward her. "Why don't we start looking on the dance floor?" He reached out to take her arm, and Shelley stepped back out of reach.

"No. I'm leaving now, anyway." She spun around on her heel and hurried through the crowd toward the door, escaping into the parking lot with a sigh of relief. Joel was going to have a lot to answer for when she finally caught up with him!

The next two locations proved much the same: boisterous, rowdy crowds of beer and whiskey drinkers, rows of amusement games, protective bartenders and no sign of her quarry. How much longer was Joel going to string this game out?

By the time she reached the next place on the list, Shelley was getting to know the rules fairly well. She walked through the door and headed straight for the bar to announce her presence to the man behind it.

"I'm Shelley Banning, and I'm looking for Joel Cassidy," she said clearly, ignoring the interested stares from the two men sitting on the bar stools beside her.

"Been expectin' you." The bartender chuckled, wiping a glass on a cloth. "Have a look around. You won't have no trouble here."

By now Shelley knew better than to try to save herself some time by asking the man whether Joel was in the tavern. The bartenders were all playing on the opposite team. She turned her back to the bar and faced the

roomful of dancers, drinkers and amusement-game players. The place was like most of the others she had been to
this evening. Thick clouds of smoke hung in the air, bold
glances swept her rounded figure and there were several
offers to buy her a drink. Across the room under a
hanging lamp there was a pool table and beyond it a
bank of video games and pinball machines.

Automatically, she narrowed her eyes to peer through
the smoky haze and scan the line of players for a lean,
redheaded male. And then she caught her breath and
stiffened. Halfway along the row of machines, the eerie
glow of a video screen reflected a familiar red flame. Joel
was here.

For a moment, Shelley simply stood quite still, not
knowing what to do next. She had been full of plans for
an angry confrontation. Her temper had been building
since he had started her off on this crazy game of
hide-and-seek, and she was sure her first words to him
were going to make her sound like a first-class shrew.
She'd had every intention of reading him the riot act
before she gave him what he sought.

But now she was frozen with suspense. With an effort
of will, she pulled herself away from the bar and started
toward the row of amusement machines. As she approached, her gaze glued to the man playing the video
game in the middle of the row, her mind whirled. What
was she going to say first? How hard was he going to
make this for her?

She was about ten feet behind him when he apparently saw her reflection on the screen in front of him. Shelley
came to a halt as he turned to face her, leaning back
against the control panel of the game. For a few seconds,
they faced each other in silence, and she was fiercely
aware of the curious combination of satisfaction and
hunger in the steel-blue eyes.

"Well, cowboy," she drawled above the racket of the

nearby machines, "have you had enough game playing tonight?"

"Can't say for sure," he responded sardonically, eyes gleaming. "Game's not quite over yet."

"Take my word for it," she told him with a cool assurance she was far from feeling. "For you, it's over."

"Yeah? Who won?"

Shelley swallowed, trying to maintain her air of nonchalance. She was aware of some of the interested glances being directed her way now. "Isn't it obvious?"

"I like to see the final score spelled out very clearly," Joel informed her evenly. He crossed his arms and waited, every inch of him singing with male challenge.

Shelley reacted to that challenge with a violent wave of emotion that seemed to span the spectrum of feminine response. Her chin came up, her hazel eyes flashed gold and her hands went to her hips in defiance.

"Joel Cassidy, you are the most annoying, aggravating, irritating man I have ever met in my life! You play games when the stakes are much too high, and then you have your own set of rules and expect me to play by them. You have run me ragged tonight chasing you from one damn bar to another. By rights I should empty that can of beer you're holding over your red head! You have no right to push me, but you're doing it, anyway. In fact, there are a lot of rights you seem to have assumed lately which you never asked for politely. Lucky for you I'm such a good-tempered, understanding, *trusting* woman or I would probably be trying to break that video game over your chauvinistic skull!"

"*Trusting?*" he interrupted her to question in a low, husky voice. The blue gaze was lighting once more with steel-turned-platinum. He didn't move, but she could feel the tautness in him. It fairly sizzled across the space between them, enveloping her and feeding her own inner tension.

"Trusting!" she repeated vengefully. "I trust you, Joel Cassidy. I would trust you to the ends of the earth. I will come and live with you if that's what you want. But I warn you, I will not play tonight's little game with you ever again! I have been in places I would normally never set foot in! I have breathed more cigarette smoke, seen more drunken cowboys, looked at more of those damn pinball and video games than I ever wish to encounter again in my life. You will come home with me now and stop this nonsense before I am forced to kick you where it will have some effect and drag you out by your heels. Do I make myself clearly understood?"

The platinum in his eyes was glowing with blue flame. The slow, lazily wicked grin was carving its way across his hard features, revealing the charmingly crooked tooth as Joel dropped his hands and straightened away from the video-game console. Shelley could feel the happiness in him, and it neutralized the frustrated temper in her. She stared at him as hungrily as he was staring at her, longing to throw herself into his arms.

"Oh, yes, Shelley, honey, you make yourself very well understood. I've told you all along that I understand you. Come and take me home. I'm tired of playing games tonight."

He held out his arms, and Shelley hurled herself into them with a small cry of happiness and relief. She could hear the laughter and the teasing remarks being made all around her, but she buried her face in Joel's blue work shirt and ignored them. His arms closed around her with a fierce possession that told her more about his own state of mind than words ever could have conveyed.

"My God, sweetheart, I was so afraid you wouldn't come after me," he rasped into her hair. "So afraid. Don't worry, I won't ever play this particular game again. Much too hard on a man's nerves! Do you really want me? Really trust me? Completely?"

She raised her head, her eyes full of the truth. "Yes! Oh, yes, Joel. I'm accustomed to having the facts neatly arranged in front of me before I make sweeping statements, but I don't need to see the numbers this time. I'm very sure of the important things tonight."

"Shelley!" He hugged her close amid the noise of the machines, the juke box and the raucous laughter. "Thank you, sweetheart! Thank you for that. My God, woman, you've given me so much tonight, I don't know how to even the score!"

Shelley's arms tightened around his waist. "You could get me out of here for starters," she teased tenderly. And sometime in the future, she added with silent resolve, you can tell me that you love me as much as I love you.

He smiled with shaky humor. "You mean accountants aren't prepared to rescue their clients from places like this?"

"We prefer to spend our time rescuing clients from the IRS," she informed him in heartfelt tones as he loosened his hold on her and caught her wrist.

He threw back his head and laughed. "Come along, Shelley, honey. I'm starving to death after all this excitement, and you must be just as hungry. Let's go find us some food!" He forged a path through the crowd toward the door, lifting a hand in farewell to the grinning bartender, and in another moment they were safely outside in the parking lot.

"I'll tell you what," he said, walking her toward her car. "You drive straight home, and I'll stop along the way for some carry-out tacos or a pizza. Okay?"

"Okay." She smiled tremulously at him, not concerned with the food, only with the feelings she was experiencing. Then she got into her car without another word and started the engine.

The white Maserati pulled into her drive about twenty

minutes after Shelley had arrived. She went to the door to meet him and found him carrying a large pizza.

"The Kitchen Sink," he explained as her eyes went to the huge, flat box.

"I beg your pardon?"

"I ordered the Kitchen Sink. That's the one with everything on it. Hungry?"

"No," she said from force of habit even though she could feel the hunger pangs starting already. The carrot sticks she'd eaten hours before hadn't lasted long, and she'd been exerting a great deal of energy since she'd eaten them. She eyed the box as he carried it through the door and on into the kitchen.

"Lucky for you I never take no for an answer from you," he growled in soft laughter. "You'd starve to death." He set the pizza down and began searching through the cupboards for plates and forks.

She watched him, unprotesting even when he cut her a huge slice and handed the plate across the counter to her. She loved him, Shelley thought. She would have gone into a hundred more bars to find him. The realization was mind twisting.

Joel came around from behind the counter and smiled down into her bemused eyes as he led the way over to the table. Shelley was suddenly aware that he still looked a little dazed himself.

"So you trust me now, hmmm?" he questioned gently as they sat down.

"Yes. I trust you, Joel. You're a clever businessman, and I think you could be quite ruthless under certain circumstances, but I don't believe you'd use me. I don't believe you would seduce me and try to bribe me and manipulate Ackerly through me." She busied herself taking a large bite from the still-hot pizza.

"Even though I know the California group is interested

in that land and even though I've never had serious objections to making the occasional half million?'' he pressed, watching her eat with a certain satisfaction.

"Even though," she agreed, nodding.

"I don't think that last bit was very good English." He chuckled.

"Accountants are more interested in numbers than grammar," she told him blandly, taking another bite.

He grinned again, and for a moment there was an aura of male satisfaction about him. A couple of bites later, Joel broke the companionable silence to ask, "Did you have any trouble tonight?"

"You mean, was I accosted? Assaulted? Did I have to fend off heavy-handed cowboys who'd had too much to drink? Dragged out onto dance floors against my will?"

Joel's pleasant expression went abruptly hard. "I left instructions for the bartenders to watch out for you!" he grated roughly.

Shelley blinked at him innocently.

"Damn it, Shelley, if anyone laid a hand on you, I'll have his hide!"

Shelley relented. "Forget it, Joel. No one made too much of a pest out of himself. Everyone was playing by your rules tonight. Including me."

He eyed her narrowly for a moment and then relaxed visibly. "Good." He took another bite out of his pizza and chewed reflectively. "When can you move in with me?"

"As soon as you like." She was truly in an accommodating mood tonight, Shelley thought wryly. Playing by his rules.

"Good," he said again with great satisfaction. "We'll arrange things tomorrow."

"Tomorrow I'm going to be tied up all day with that Ackerly audit," she reminded him. "It may take two or three days to find what I'm looking for. I shall probably be exhausted after work."

"Too exhausted to worry about moving, huh?" he said blandly.

"Probably." Shelley felt a tinge of wariness invade the pleasant, intimate atmosphere between them. She put down her slice of pizza and looked at him steadily. "But I will start packing tonight if that's what you want, Joel. Practically speaking, it would be easier to wait until I've cleared up the Ackerly thing, but if you want me to come sooner, I will."

His eyes cleared, and a small smile tugged at his lips. "That's all right," he returned offhandedly. "I'll just move in with you until you're ready to pack up and come live with me. Starting tonight."

She nodded silently, glancing down at her pizza, then back up again as he suddenly reached across the table and trapped her fingers beneath his large, competent hand. "It's not that I don't trust you, Shelley," he explained very coolly. "I've said I do, and that's the truth."

"Then why . . . ?"

"Because you mentioned something about a bribe," he said simply. "Shelley, people who resort to bribes will sometimes resort to other methods of intimidation. I think it's best that you don't spend any more nights alone. I wish you'd told me right away about that phone call you got," he added thoughtfully.

It was her turn to relax a little. "So you're only moving in with me tonight to protect me from possible threats of violence and intimidation?" She chuckled.

"That's about all I *can* protect you from tonight." He grinned wickedly. "I took my shaving kit home this morning, and I'm afraid it's still there."

She grinned back at him, feeling inordinately light-hearted. "So much for your foresight and planning!"

"As it happens, you're going to need all the rest you can get, anyway, for that audit tomorrow, aren't you?" he retorted smoothly. "And something tells me we've both had enough exercise for one evening. Tonight we go to bed and go to sleep."

"And tomorrow night?" she taunted, her eyes full of laughter.

"Tomorrow night I won't have as much on my mind as I did tonight. I'll remember the shaving kit!" he promised firmly.

10

Joel was waiting for Shelley when she finally got home after the first day of the massive audit. Taking one look at her drooping posture and exhausted eyes, he handed her a drink, fixed dinner and put her to bed. She curled in his arms and fell asleep as soon as her head touched the pillow. Her last thought before closing her eyes was a sense of wonder at the luxury of being cosseted by Joel Cassidy.

The second day of the audit went much the same as the first, but by the end of the day, Shelley knew she had found a thread. She told Joel as much as she put her feet on the recliner and accepted the drink he thrust into her hand.

"Tomorrow I'll start pulling on it and see what unravels," she murmured, and then proceeded to doze off as he fixed dinner. He woke her long enough to eat and then once more put her to bed like a child.

"I really could do this by myself," she protested mildly as he undressed her and slipped the nightgown over her tousled head.

"My privilege," he said smiling.

She was up at four-thirty the next morning to start the unraveling process. By ten o'clock, she and her team were certain they had an outline of the scam, and by noon she was presenting all the facts to a stunned Dean Ackerly.

That afternoon, Shelley arrived home on time, and although she was tired, she was not experiencing the exhaustion of the two previous days. Success and satisfaction lit her eyes as she came through the front door.

"Tell me all about it," Joel ordered, handing her a drink and sinking into the chair across from her. "I can see you found what you were looking for!"

"And just in time, too. Much farther down the trail and nothing would have helped Ackerly! Not even another couple of hundred-thousand-dollar interest-free loans from you!" Shelley shook her head, still faintly disbelieving. "It was a complicated scheme by one of Dean's most trusted managers. Thousands of dollars' worth of merchandise was supposedly being shipped every few months to a customer who wasn't paying his bills. In reality, the customer was involved in the scheme. He received the merchandise, turned around and disposed of it for cash, kept a percentage and sent the rest back to the manager."

Joel arched one red brow and took a sip of his drink. "Not bad. The manager conceals the fact that more and more merchandise is being shipped without being paid for and continues to pocket the cash the so-called customer is getting for the goods. Over a period of time, that would put one hell of a drain on any firm's cash flow."

Shelley grinned at him disparagingly. "You don't have to sound so admiring!"

"Never let it be said I can't appreciate a well-constructed—"

"Game?" she supplied before he could finish the sentence.

"Or a well-constructed game player," he retorted easily, his eyes roving blatantly over her rounded figure.

In spite of herself, Shelley blushed, covering the temporary loss of composure with a long sip of her cool drink. "In any event, it's over now."

"Justice prevails?"

"Almost." She grimaced. "Unfortunately, at about the time my staff and I were starting to get it all put together, the manager in question realized the good times were over. When I went in to Dean with the facts, it was discovered that the man behind the scheme had reported sick for the day. By the time they tracked him down, he was on a plane to Mexico. We might be able to get the supposed 'customer' who was in charge of disposing of the goods, but it's doubtful. And we'll probably never learn who he hired to make the phone call to me. White-collar crime is difficult to prosecute. The best way of handling it is to stop it at the source by having good security measures in place such as regular audits."

"Sounds like the accounting department at Ackerly Manufacturing needs a few internal procedural changes, too," Joel drawled.

Shelley nodded in agreement. "Lots of work at Ackerly for a good consulting accountant," she said pleasantly.

"Lots of work at Cassidy & Co., too. You're going to be busy, Shelley."

"I certainly will," she said with a note of satisfaction. She glanced down at the drink in her hand. "I shall miss all the pampering after a hard day's work, though. I assume this luxury of having my drink and my dinner ready when I get home won't go on forever?"

He looked at her, but there was no teasing laughter in his blue eyes as she had expected. Some other emotion flickered there, an emotion that made Shelley tighten her fingers around the glass in her hand.

"I figure we can alternate," Joel said slowly. "Some nights you can have the drinks ready, and some nights I'll have them ready. And some nights we'll fix them together." He was holding her gaze in the bonds of his own, saying something much more important with his eyes than with his words. "That way the luxury could go on forever."

"Joel—" she began tightly.

"Have you enjoyed having a husband for the past couple of days, Shelley?" he went on whimsically. "Think you could get used to the idea?"

"Joel Cassidy, this is one game I won't play with you," Shelley whispered throatily as she searched his face for the truth. "If you're asking me to marry you, then you can damn well do it properly!"

"I am trying to do it properly," he told her thickly. "It's just that I haven't had much practice."

"Oh, Joel," she said, her eyes filling with love as she shakily set down her glass. "Of course I'll marry you. I'd live with you, I'd marry you, I'd run away with you, I'd do anything for you. Don't you realize that?"

"Shelley!"

He was on his feet, pulling her up beside him and burying his face in the hair behind her ear as he held her fiercely.

"You don't have to marry me, Joel. You know that,"

she murmured unevenly into his shoulder as she wrapped her arms around his waist and clung. "I don't have a particularly good track record where marriage is concerned and I—"

"Just tell me that you love me," he ordered huskily, "and the hell with the rest."

"I love you," she replied obediently. "I love you more than I thought I would ever love any man or any thing."

He pulled back a short distance to cradle her face between rough palms. His blue eyes burned down at her. "Shelley, I love you. I've never felt like this with anyone else. I was going to wait until I had you safely living under my roof, and then I was going to systematically seduce you until you fell in love with me before I asked you to marry me. But tonight, after the past couple of days of worrying about you, looking after you, it just slipped out. I couldn't wait any longer to ask you. I had to *know*."

"Had to know what?" she mumbled into his shirt, her heart singing, her tiredness evaporating.

"That when you moved in with me, you really would belong to me. Completely. With you I find myself wanting all the traditional commitments, all the words, all the vows. I'm a greedy man, sweetheart."

"And you like to win," she added complacently.

"With the stakes this high, I didn't dare lose," he confessed grimly.

"Were you ever in any doubt?" she teased.

"I knew I could make you want me," he said honestly. "And I knew I understood how your mind worked. I thought that would give me an edge. But love is something that isn't easily manipulated. It either exists or it doesn't, and I could only hope it would be there when I went after it."

"It's there. I knew it was there when I realized I had no choice but to trust you. It was all bound up together in one package. I could have stood in that bar the other night and yelled that I loved you as easily as I yelled that I trusted you. Same thing."

"Sweetheart!" He gathered her close, and for a long moment they simply stood there, luxuriating in the wonder of the moment.

Then Shelley's nose twitched. "Joel?"

"Ummm?"

"Is something burning?"

He stiffened. "Oh, my God! Dinner!"

Instantly, she was free as he raced for the kitchen.

Afterward, Shelley could not have said exactly what she ate, nor did she notice whether the food was slightly singed. The one thing she did remember was the glittering love in the eyes of the man who sat across from her. When dinner was over, they cleared the table together and walked into the living room.

"I have a wedding gift for you." Joel grinned, dropping her hand to move toward the puzzle table. He picked up the box that she had vaguely noticed and dismissed earlier. "Here, open it."

She unwrapped the package with smiling eyes, knowing what it was from the way it rattled. "You seem determined to seduce me with puzzles and games, Joel." She glanced down at the new jigsaw puzzle with pleasure and then back up at him. "Thank you. When it's finished, we'll have it framed!" Standing on tiptoe, she brushed her lips lightly against his.

He caught her around the waist and held her in place when she would have stepped back. Obedient to the darkening fire in his eyes, Shelley wound her arms around his neck.

"Shelley, if you hadn't found out who was really behind that bribe attempt and if you hadn't discovered what was going on at Ackerly—" he began slowly.

"I would still have been sure of you," she told him

firmly. "After all, as you keep telling me, we've got a lot in common. We understand each other. Bribery wouldn't be your style at all."

"And seduction?" he prompted.

She shook her head. "You're much too honest in bed for that to be an effective technique for you to use!"

He smiled quizzically. "Honest in bed? I like that. That's the way I found you, too. Honest. You gave yourself completely, and I was sure you couldn't be doing that and trying to use me at the same time." He bent and lifted her into his arms.

"Aren't we going to start the new puzzle?" she murmured, threading her fingers through the flame of his hair.

"We're going to work on one we've already started. I figure it's going to take the rest of our lives to get it put together properly. Just when I think we've got it completed, it explodes in my hands, you see."

"Ah, an exploding puzzle." She nodded wisely. "Tricky."

"Very. But infinitely interesting," he whispered as he carried her into the bedroom and set her down on her feet beside the bed. "Infinitely intriguing," he added, finding her mouth with his own as his hands went to the fastenings of her clothes.

They undressed each other in loving silence, letting the clothing fall unheeded to the floor at their feet. Then they stood in the shadowy room and touched each other with a sense of wonder and joy that Shelley knew would return to them again and again down through the years. She felt her full breasts grow taut beneath Joel's fingers, knew the planes of his chest as she ran her fingertips down to his waist.

When he picked her up again and settled her in the middle of the turned-back bed, Shelley sighed with the longing and the need he aroused in her. For a moment, he stood looking down at her as if assuring himself that she was for real, and then, with a muffled exclamation, Joel lowered himself to the bed beside her, pulling her into his arms with barely controlled need.

"Shelley, my sweet love."

His hands moved over her, gently rasping the tips of her breasts, drawing teasing circles on her stomach, finding the sensitive area at the base of her spine.

When she arched lovingly against him, he buried his lips in her throat. "Touch me, my love," he begged.

She let her fingertips find the line of his rib cage and then the muscular planes of his hips. Slowly, she stroked the strong thighs, moaning softly when his own hands clenched abruptly into her hips in reaction.

"Oh, God, Shelley!"

He parted her legs with his hand and feathered the inside of her thigh. Higher and higher he traced the enticing patterns until she was stirring with the deepest of longings. As his fingers found the burning heart of her, his teeth gently caught hold of a nipple, savaging it with unbelievable care until it throbbed.

"Joel!"

"You take my breath away," he whispered.

They stoked the flames in each other higher and higher, exploring every intimate place, claiming each sensual frontier. Shelley's breath came in tiny moans of love and need, and her body arched again and again at his touch.

At last he came to her in a surging rush of power and desire that brought a gasping cry from Shelley's lips. Her body accepted the loving invasion as perfectly as if he were the other half of a human puzzle. Together they made a wondrously complete being.

The pattern of their passion built into a raging crescendo, sweeping all before it. Shelley's nails bit deeply into the hard contour of Joel's shoulders, and he growled an answering response, then nipped at the soft skin above her breast until she thought she would lose her senses. The excitement of their union was a captivating, thrilling thing that summoned all her senses toward the inevitable explosion of delight.

"Oh, Joel, yes! Yes!"

He caught her hips more tightly against his own, and she wrapped her legs around his waist as he filled her unbearably full. Her passion fired his own, and Shelley knew a primitive delight in being able to arouse him so violently, in having him take her so completely.

At last, the rippling pleasure began, unwinding with sizzling suddenness from deep inside her. Joel reacted to the tiny shivers of her body with a husky gasp, and then he, too, succumbed. Together they clung during the ensuing explosion, holding fast to each other as the universe stretched taut around them and then collapsed inward.

"When," Joel demanded a long time later, "are you going to marry me?"

Shelley curled against him, her eyes soft and glowing. "When would you like me to marry you?"

"As soon as it's legally possible," he stated categorically.

"A man of decision," she said admiringly.

He shook his head once. "Just a man who likes to get all the loose ends of a business deal sewn up completely."

"All the pieces of the puzzle put together?" she clarified indulgently.

"Exactly." He grinned with satisfaction. "How many times does a man have an opportunity to marry his accountant?"

"I wouldn't know, but it does sound like a good business practice. Think of the unparalleled possibilities for keeping track of your finances!"

"Ummm. In great detail," he agreed. "Speaking of which, there's a hundred thousand dollars of my money for which I'm still holding you responsible."

"I was going to mention that a bit later."

"Uh huh." His eyes gleamed suspiciously through the auburn lashes. "When I was feeling suitably accommodating?"

"Something like that. How would you feel about letting Ackerly sell that land to the California group and paying you off out of the proceeds? With interest, of course."

"Don't you know I'm a sucker for a fast little hustler like yourself?" He sighed. "You could talk me into anything. The Brooklyn Bridge, swampland in Florida—"

"Joel," she said very seriously. "I don't want to fast-talk you into this. If you don't like the deal, I'll work out something else with Ackerly. Now that we've plugged the leak, we can get things back on the right track without having to sell that land."

"I don't care what you do." He chuckled. "Just so I get what's coming to me. A hundred thousand dollars plus interest plus you will suit me fine, sweetheart!"

"Plus me?" she repeated, her eyes laughing up at him.

"I," he declared blandly, "am considered a very shrewd bargainer."

"I understand," she murmured, lifting a fingertip to toy with the curling hair on his chest. "A real hustler."

"Two of a kind, aren't we?" he drawled, turning on his side with sudden intention and leaning forward to kiss the peak of her breast.

"Yes."

He lifted his head. "You agree? Finally?"

"Yes." She smiled up at him with love and understanding. "I won't say I like the word itself, but I suppose it's the truth."

"There's nothing wrong with the word," he told her firmly. "Being a pair of hustlers will assure us of two very important things in our old age."

"What important things?" she teased as he lazily trailed a palm down to her thigh.

"We shall be rich, for one thing," he said against the skin of her stomach.

"And for another?"

"We shall understand each other. Add those things to the indisputable fact that we love each other and we'll make out like bandits!"

"I'm inclined to agree." She drew in her breath as he nibbled deliciously at her thigh. "Joel, I do love you."

"I know. I love you."

"I know. Now I know. You might hustle me, but you'd never lie to me, would you?"

"No." Then he chuckled.

"What's so funny?" she demanded, stirring languidly beneath his increasingly intense touch.

"I was thinking about the truth in the old saying that there are three people in the world to whom a smart man never lies: his doctor, his lawyer and—"

"And his accountant," Shelley finished on a note of laughter.

"I'm a smart man."

"I've never doubted it. Darling, what are you doing?"

"Isn't it obvious?"

"But we just did! I mean, so soon? Again?"

"Trust me," he whispered, covering her mouth with his own.

Shelley did.

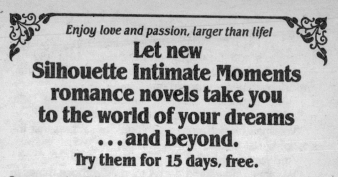

YOU'LL BE SWEPT AWAY
WITH SILHOUETTE DESIRE

$1.75 each

1 ☐ CORPORATE AFFAIR
James

2 ☐ LOVE'S SILVER WEB
Monet

3 ☐ WISE FOLLY
Clay

4 ☐ KISS AND TELL
Carey

5 ☐ WHEN LAST WE LOVED
Baker

6 ☐ A FRENCHMAN'S KISS
Mallory

7 ☐ NOT EVEN FOR LOVE
St. Claire

8 ☐ MAKE NO PROMISES
Dee

9 ☐ MOMENT IN TIME
Simms

10 ☐ WHENEVER I LOVE YOU
Smith

$1.95 each

11 ☐ VELVET TOUCH
James

12 ☐ THE COWBOY AND THE
LADY   Palmer

13 ☐ COME BACK, MY LOVE
Wallace

14 ☐ BLANKET OF STARS
Valley

15 ☐ SWEET BONDAGE
Vernon

16 ☐ DREAM COME TRUE
Major

19 ☐ LOVER IN PURSUIT
James

20 ☐ KING OF DIAMONDS
Allison

21 ☐ LOVE IN THE CHINA SEA
Baker

22 ☐ BITTERSWEET IN BERN
Durant

23 ☐ CONSTANT STRANGER
Sunshine

24 ☐ SHARED MOMENTS
Baxter

25 ☐ RENAISSANCE MAN
James

26 ☐ SEPTEMBER MORNING
Palmer

27 ☐ ON WINGS OF NIGHT
Conrad

28 ☐ PASSIONATE JOURNEY
Lovan

29 ☐ ENCHANTED DESERT
Michelle

30 ☐ PAST FORGETTING
Lind

31 ☐ RECKLESS PASSION
James

32 ☐ YESTERDAY'S DREAMS
Clay

38 ☐ SWEET SERENITY
Douglass

39 ☐ SHADOW OF BETRAYAL
Monet

40 ☐ GENTLE CONQUEST
Mallory

41 ☐ SEDUCTION BY DESIGN
St. Claire

Silhouette Desire

42 ☐ ASK ME NO SECRETS Stewart	59 ☐ TIME STANDS STILL Powers
43 ☐ A WILD, SWEET MAGIC Simms	60 ☐ BETWEEN THE LINES Dennis
44 ☐ HEART OVER MIND West	61 ☐ ALL THE NIGHT LONG Simms
45 ☐ EXPERIMENT IN LOVE Clay	62 ☐ PASSIONATE SILENCE Monet
46 ☐ HER GOLDEN EYES Chance	
47 ☐ SILVER PROMISES Michelle	63 ☐ SHARE YOUR TOMORROWS Dee
48 ☐ DREAM OF THE WEST Powers	64 ☐ SONATINA Milan
49 ☐ AFFAIR OF HONOR James	65 ☐ RECKLESS VENTURE Allison
50 ☐ FRIENDS AND LOVERS Palmer	66 ☐ THE FIERCE GENTLENESS Langtry
51 ☐ SHADOW OF THE MOUNTAIN Lind	67 ☐ GAMEMASTER James
52 ☐ EMBERS OF THE SUN Morgan	68 ☐ SHADOW OF YESTERDAY Browning
53 ☐ WINTER LADY Joyce	69 ☐ PASSION'S PORTRAIT Carey
54 ☐ IF EVER YOU NEED ME Fulford	70 ☐ DINNER FOR TWO Victor
55 ☐ TO TAME THE HUNTER James	71 ☐ MAN OF THE HOUSE Joyce
56 ☐ FLIP SIDE OF YESTERDAY Douglass	72 ☐ NOBODY'S BABY Hart
57 ☐ NO PLACE FOR A WOMAN Michelle	
58 ☐ ONE NIGHT'S DECEPTION Mallory	

SILHOUETTE DESIRE, Department SD/6
1230 Avenue of the Americas
New York, NY 10020

Please send me the books I have checked above. I am enclosing $_____
(please add 50¢ to cover postage and handling. NYS and NYC residents please add
appropriate sales tax.) Send check or money order—no cash or C.O.D.'s please.
Allow six weeks for delivery.

NAME _____

ADDRESS _____

CITY _____ STATE/ZIP _____